Praise for *Sidetracked*

ABA Indies Introduce title
ALSC Notable Children's Book

"Heartwarming and funny, *Sidetracked* is the book we all wish we had read in seventh grade." —Gitty Daneshvari, author of *School of Fear* and *The League of Unexceptional Children*

"Just read it! Diana Harmon Asher has written a witty, observant, and sensitive novel."
—Susan Isaacs, *New York Times* bestselling author

"Joseph's first-person voice is fresh and authentic, and his character arc is immensely satisfying."
—*Kirkus Reviews*

"The characters in Asher's debut novel are likable and approachable, and the story is absorbing and moves quickly."
—*School Library Journal*

"Natural-sounding narrative with a good amount of humor."
—*The Horn Book*

"Joseph's first-person narrative engages readers on page one and never lets up."
—*Booklist*

CKED

Diana Harmon Asher

Amulet Books
New York

Library of Congress Cataloging-in-Publication Data

Names: Asher, Diana Harmon.
Title: Sidetracked / by Diana Harmon Asher.
Description: New York : Amulet Books, 2017. | Summary: "Seventh-grader Joseph Friedman is friendless and puny, with ADD to boot. He spends most of his time avoiding the class bully and hiding out in the Resource Room. But the Resource Room teacher encourages (i.e., practically forces) him to join the school cross country team, and he meets Heather, a new student who's tough and athletic and refuses to be pushed around by anybody"—Provided by publisher.
Identifiers: LCCN 2016052084 (print) | LCCN 2017004537 (ebook) | ISBN 978-1-6833-5120-7 (ebook) | ISBN 978-1-4197-2601-9 (alk. paper)
Subjects: | CYAC: Friendship—Fiction. | Running—Fiction. | Bullying—Fiction. | Learning disabilities—Fiction. | Attention-deficit hyperactivity disorder—Fiction. | Middle school—Fiction. | Schools—Fiction. | Jews—United States—Fiction.
Classification: LCC PZ7.1.A83 (ebook) | LCC PZ7.1.A83 Fr 2017 (print) | DDC [Fic]—dc23
LC record available at https://lccn.loc.gov/2016052084

Paperback ISBN: 978-1-4197-3139-6

Originally published in hardcover by Amulet Books in 2017
Text copyright © 2017 Diana Harmon Asher
Cover illustration copyright © 2018 Tim Tierney
Book design by Siobhán Gallagher

Printed and bound in U.S.A.
10 9 8 7 6 5
Amulet Books are available at special discounts when purchased in quantity for premiums and promotions as well as fundraising or educational use. Special editions can also be created to specification. For details, contact specialsales@abramsbooks.com or the address below.

Amulet Books® is a registered trademark of Harry N. Abrams, Inc.

ABRAMS The Art of Books
195 Broadway, New York, NY 10007
abramsbooks.com

For my mother.

–DA

CHAPTER 1

"FRIEDMAN!"

I open my eyes and look up. It's Coach DeSalvo and he's trudging my way.

"Me?" I say.

Coach DeSalvo stops in front of me. He folds his arms and looks around the soccer field. "I don't see any other Friedmans here," he says.

That's not strictly true. There's Tiffany Freedman, but she spells it with two "E"s, and she's a girl.

"Friedman," he says again, "what are you doing back there?"

"Um . . . playing defense?" I answer.

"From behind the goal?" I look at the net. Yup. It's clearly in front of me. "What's the matter with you, anyway, Friedman? What are you afraid of?"

I want to say, "Green olives with red speckled tongues." I want to say, "Stewed prunes and vampire bats and street sweepers." I want to say, "Charlie Kastner," who just a minute ago was charging toward me with a crazed look that I've seen

in the eyes of a raging buffalo on Animal Planet, which is why I've ended up crouched behind the goal, covering my head with my hands, during our first PE class of seventh grade.

But instead, I just say, "Nothing."

"Nothing. Good." Coach DeSalvo walks around the net, plants a meaty hand in the middle of my back, and guides me to a spot near the middle of the field. "Then pick it up, Friedman. Stop running away from the ball."

All this has made my stomach shake, but I manage to say, "Okay."

Coach DeSalvo marches over to the other side of the field. He blows his whistle and the game starts up again.

"Frank," I say to Frank Maldonado, "am I on your team?"

He looks at me like he's not sure if I'm kidding. I'm not.

"Yes. Unfortunately," he says.

"How can you tell?" I ask.

"Pinnies?" he says, like it's a question I should know the answer to.

I look around. Half the kids are wearing those little blue bibs. "Oh. Yeah," I say. "Thanks."

I try to move around like the other kids, in case Coach DeSalvo is watching, but, not surprisingly, he's forgotten all about me. I drift over toward the sideline, where a gray squirrel is hunting around in that herky-jerky squirrelly way. I watch how he picks up a fat brown maple seed—the kind with wings that looks like an angel. He clutches it in his pointy little squirrel hands, turning it around and around to find just the right biting-in place.

Then all of a sudden he freezes. He sits up straight, staring at a spot right behind me.

I freeze too, feeling the earth shake under me. I turn to see what's causing it: twenty-four sets of middle school feet charging down the field. And out in front is Charlie Kastner, dribbling the soccer ball like a maniac and heading straight for me.

This time, there's nowhere to run. All I can do is brace for impact and hope to heal up by Thanksgiving.

But instead of being smashed and ground to dust, I watch as Charlie's legs fly miraculously out from under him. His big sweaty body tumbles through the air. It seems like an eternity that he's up there, and then he lands with a thud on the grass. Someone has taken out Charlie Kastner and stolen the ball!

It's a girl.

She's by me in a flash, passing so close that her hair slaps me across the face. It's not tied back in a ponytail like the other girls'. It's flying wild. The ball skips ahead of her, celebrating its rescue from Charlie's clutches. All the other kids—whose thundering feet would have trampled my remains if Charlie had mowed me down—make a U-turn, following this new girl, as she dribbles the ball back toward the other team's goal.

Charlie gives me a vengeful look, then gets up and runs after the girl, but there's no way he can catch her. She's big—not fat, but tall and strong. And she's fast—faster than the boys, faster than everybody.

She's down the field now and the only one with a chance to stop her is Billy Hayward. He's small and wiry, and he's stayed back to guard the goal. He sticks out his leg to steal the ball or trip her up, or both, but she gives him a nudge with her hip—the same nudge she must have given Charlie—and Billy is launched three feet in the air. It's as if a tornado picks him up, twirls him around, and plunks him back down again.

The boys stop in their tracks, staring. The girls glare at this new girl, because they like Billy, and they don't want to see him tossed in the air like a Hacky Sack. Sally MacNamara, the goalie, is sending out vibes of mortal terror now that Billy, her last line of defense, is down. She doesn't even take a step toward the ball as it flies into the net.

It's a goal, but nobody cheers.

Coach De Salvo blows his whistle. "What's everybody staring at?" he calls out. Nobody says anything, but the answer is obvious. Even I know they're staring at the new girl, and if anybody's not going to be clued in, it's me. "Haven't you ever seen a hip check before?"

"It has a name?" mutters Billy.

"Jeez," adds his friend Zachary.

"Young lady," says Coach DeSalvo, "I hope you'll be trying out for the girls' soccer team."

"She belongs on the football team," says Billy.

"She belongs on the Godzilla team," says Zachary, and all the boys laugh.

The tall girl shrugs and looks at the ground. Her sandy-colored hair falls forward so I can't see much of her face. It occurs to me that Coach DeSalvo could put a hand on her shoulder and introduce her, since she's new and doesn't know anybody, but he doesn't. Instead, he blows his whistle again, points to the gym door, and tosses the ball to Charlie to carry in. And, I guess because he has to reestablish his rank in our seventh-grade world, Charlie calls my name and fakes a hard throw right at me. He doesn't even have to let go of the ball. He just holds it over his head and jerks it forward, and I instinctively duck, triggering a wave of laughter.

The crowd separates into boys and girls. The girls are whispering to each other, and the boys are crashing in through the back door, racing for the water fountain.

Trailing the girls is the new girl. Trailing the boys is me.

CHAPTER 2

MY MOUTH FEELS LIKE A SANDPIT, BUT I DON'T get in line at the gym water fountain. There are trade-offs you have to make in middle school, and sandpit mouth beats whatever Charlie has in mind for me any day. Fortunately, someone knew enough to give us LD kids our own water fountain outside the Resource Room, my next-period class.

LD stands for "learning differences." It used to stand for "learning disabilities," before they decided to make us sound a little less tragic. The Resource Room is where LD kids go to get organized, catch up, and not get yelled at so much.

Everyone in the Resource Room has "issues," or as my mother says, "stuff" that gets in the way. Mine is ADD— attention deficit disorder. ADD is a lot like ADHD, which might be even worse, because that "H" stands for "hyperactivity," meaning you have way too much energy for your own good. My "H" isn't really so bad, though, so I'm just ADD.

People think having ADD means I can't focus, but that's not really true. I focus very well—just on the wrong things.

Instead of hearing the assignment, I'm watching a ladybug crawl along the windowsill. When I'm supposed to be reading the chapter in our textbook called "Changes Down the Road: The Assembly Line," I'm staring at the head-on picture of a Model T, thinking how it looks like my great-uncle Herman. Also, I flinch at loud sounds, can't fit my writing between the lines, and hate the feel of scratchy wool, but I don't know if that's the ADD or something else altogether.

For me, every day in middle school is a little bit like the Running of the Bulls. That's something I saw on TV that happens in a place called Pamplona, in Spain. Once a year, they let a whole herd of bulls out free in the streets, and people try to outrun them, or else duck into a back alley to avoid being gored to death. That's kind of how I feel. I try to keep up, or stay out of the way, or find someplace to hide.

My back alley is the Resource Room. My teacher here is Mrs. T. Her real name is Mrs. Teitelbaum, but she likes "Mrs. T" better. She's an upbeat person who dances down the "extra help hallway," singing songs like "All the Single Ladies." I know she's married, though, because she has a picture of her husband on the wall by her desk, along with her two dogs, George and Ringo.

Mrs. T likes polka dots and the color pink. Her hair is short and a little spiky and she has a habit of running her fingers through it. Sometimes she just forgets and her hand stays perched up there, making her look confused, or, when she wears pink, like an upside-down flamingo.

After gym I take about ten gulps of water at the Resource Room fountain and come in to see Mrs. T in just that position. She's holding the daily bulletin in one hand, with the other one on top of her head. She reads the bulletin out loud to us every day to make sure nothing important gets by us, and, trust me, it would.

"Attention, journalists," Mrs. T begins as I plop into my seat. "Come to a meeting on September fifteenth in Room D-1. Our monthly paper, *The Inkwell*, needs writers to report the news you want to know!"

I try to imagine what *The Inkwell* would look like if it really did report the news kids wanted to know. The headline today would be TALL GIRL COMES TO LAKEVIEW! OUTPLAYS LOCAL BULLY!! It would tell where she came from and what her name was and how she knew that my life was in mortal danger at that very moment.

Danielle Symington volunteers for *The Inkwell,* and Mrs. T says, "Excellent, Danielle," takes her hand down from its perch on her head, and writes on the board in purple, "Danielle: Sept. 15 — *Inkwell* meeting."

She goes on reading. "The Spanish Club will meet on

Tuesday, September thirteenth, in Señora Finnegan's room at three fifteen. No Spanish necessary."

"But it's a Spanish club," says Danielle, who seems way too together to be in the Resource Room. "How can there be no Spanish necessary?"

"Maybe you'll learn about Spain's beautiful culture," suggests Mrs. T. "Dancing, music . . ."

"I speak Spanish," says Trevor Holcombe, who's sitting on a bookcase. "*Taco, burrito, gordita* . . ."

"*Nachos, chalupas, enchiladas*," adds Sanjit Chaudary, which sets off a flood of "*fajitas*" and "*tamales*" and "*chimichangas*," and makes me think of the Running of the Bulls again.

"Okay! Enough," says Mrs. T, but she waits patiently until we've run down the entire list of Taco Bell menu items.

"Moving on," she says in a loud voice. "This is important. The renovation of our middle-school track is complete. Lakeview athletics will now include a seventh-grade track and cross country team. Let's get Lakeview running! Come to a meeting after school tomorrow, Friday, September ninth, in Room D-5."

"Running isn't a sport," says Trevor. He's swinging his heels and they bang the shelves of the bookcase with a *thunk, thunk.*

"What do you mean, it's not a sport?" says Mrs. T. "And get down off the bookcase, please, Trevor."

"I mean it's not a real sport, like basketball or football," says Trevor.

"Like you're the quarterback?" mutters Sanjit.

"Running is stupid," adds Trevor, just to make sure we all get it. He jumps off the bookcase, knocking a copy of *Joey Pigza Swallowed the Key* to the floor.

"It certainly is not stupid!" says Mrs. T. "It would be great for all of you." And then, for some completely crazy reason, she looks at me. "Joseph," she says, "this is exactly the kind of thing that you should try."

"Me?" I say. "I'm terrible at sports."

"Don't be negative, Joseph. You can run. I know you can."

"Yeah, away from the ball," mutters Trevor.

"I'm the slowest kid in the grade," I say.

Sanjit nods. "Really, Mrs. T. He's not kidding."

"You don't have to be fast," says Mrs. T. "You start slow and get faster. Running is something you can do your whole life."

"But I can't..." I start, but I know right away it's a mistake. She stares me down.

"We don't say 'can't' here, Joseph. We take things step by step and..."

"We believe in ourselves," I fill in halfheartedly, because it's kind of Mrs. T's motto.

"So how about the rest of you? Who'll go to the meeting?"

Sanjit raises his hand. "I like to run. I'll go." Sanjit really likes Mrs. T and always tries to be agreeable.

"Me, too," says Erica Chen. I think she likes Sanjit a little bit.

"Excellent!" says Mrs. T. She writes down Sanjit and Erica's names. "Joseph?"

"Go on, Joseph," say Danielle and Trevor, in a way that I sense is not completely supportive, but I'm never really sure about things like that.

I have no good excuse. It's not like I take clarinet lessons or do judo or anything. Most of my afternoons are spent trying to do my homework and getting frustrated and distracted, or distracted and frustrated, depending on the day. Sometimes I watch nature shows, but I turn them off when something's about to get killed.

Also, I worry. I worry a lot.

But Mrs. T is waiting for an answer. So even though running isn't the first thing on my To Do list—like I even have a To Do list—I say okay. I'll go to the meeting. And Mrs. T dances back over to the whiteboard and adds my name in red: "Joseph: Sept. 9 — Track Meeting, Room D-5."

CHAPTER 3

WHEN I GET HOME, I'M SURPRISED TO HEAR MY parents' voices coming from the kitchen. My dad is never home from work this early.

"What do you mean, 'in police custody'?" my mom is asking.

"That's all they said. They called and told me that he's in police custody."

"He's practically eighty years old, for heaven's sake, on a trip with Sunshine Senior Living. What could he have done?"

"I don't know," Dad says. "You know he can get ornery sometimes."

"Are you talking about Grandpa?" I ask.

They both turn to stare at me. I guess I've got quiet feet, because they get this look like I've suddenly materialized in a puff of smoke. They look at each other, and my mom says, "Grandpa's in Atlantic City."

"He got arrested?"

"Well . . ." stalls Dad.

"How did he get in trouble?" I ask. This is starting to sound really exciting.

"I don't know if he's in trouble, exactly . . ." Dad says.

"You said he's in police custody, Matt," says my mom. "He has to be in some sort of trouble."

"All I know is that the police picked him up and took him to the station."

"Are they holding him for questioning?" I ask. That's what they do on TV—hold people for questioning.

"I highly doubt that," Mom says. "He didn't rob a bank."

"At least, we don't think so," Dad mutters, giving me a wink.

"Matt . . ." Mom says in her warning tone.

"Are you going to spring him?" I ask. I've always wanted to spring someone from jail. I can see it now—the sleeping deputy, keychain dangling . . .

"Nobody's going to spring anybody," says Mom. "It's not like they have him locked up down there."

"Well, you know," my dad says, "'in police custody' pretty much means . . ."

"You mean they have him behind bars?" My mom is looking pale.

"Of course not, sweetie. Can't you tell when I'm joking?"

I don't always know when someone's joking, but I thought my mom did.

"Matt, we've got to bring him home." Mom is going around the kitchen in fast motion, picking things up, stuffing them in drawers.

"I'll go down," Dad says. "I'll bring him back in the morning. You stay here with Joseph."

"Why can't I come?" I protest, even though I know the answer.

"Because it's the first week of school. Your father can handle it," Mom says, but she doesn't look all that confident, especially since my father is now scrolling down his cell phone calendar and loosening his tie, which is what he does when he's checking his sales appointments. My dad sells dental equipment. In fact, he's such a good dental equipment salesman, he's won an award called the Golden Crown three times.

"Matt!" Mom says. "My father is in prison!"

"Okay, okay," he says, putting down his cell. He picks up the car keys and dangles them in front of my mother. "I'm going, right now. I'll change and hit the road."

When Dad goes upstairs, Mom sits down at the table and rubs her forehead. "How was school?" she asks, in a half-hearted way.

I'm about to answer with my standard "Fine," but then I remember that there is actually something to tell her. "Charlie Kastner got knocked on his butt in gym."

"That's a good place for him," says my mother.

"By a girl," I add.

"Really!" she says. "Who?"

"I don't know her name," I say. "She's new. She's taller and faster than the boys."

"Wow. That can't be easy for her," she says. I'm not sure why.

"We were playing soccer," I tell her, "and Charlie would've crashed into me in about a second, but she caught him from behind and came to my—"

Mom cuts me off when my dad appears in jeans and a T-shirt. "Matt, you're going dressed like that?"

"You want me to wear a tuxedo?"

"Shouldn't you look more respectful?"

"I don't think they care, Sheila." He takes out his wallet and looks inside. "I don't have a lot of cash. If there's bail, do you think they take credit cards?"

"Bail?"

That sends my mom back into another nervous flurry and I head to my room. "Rescue," I say to myself, finishing the thought I started in the kitchen. "She came to my rescue."

After a few minutes, Dad comes to my door. "I'll see you tomorrow," he says. "Guess I'm off to save the day."

I get up and give him a hug. Rescue seems to be in the air. I sit on my bed and picture the scene from PE one more time—that girl coming down the field, her hair so wild, the way she sent Charlie flying and landing with a thud. It makes me smile.

CHAPTER 4

THE NEXT MORNING, MOM HANGS UP THE PHONE and tells me that everything's fine. Actually, she says, "Fine. Just fine," which usually means it's really not. Or maybe it is, but she's not happy about it.

"Is Dad coming back with Grandpa?" I ask. "Is he taking him to Sunshine?"

"I think for now he'll stay with us." She sighs. "I don't know how Sunshine will feel about all this."

This could be the last straw for Grandpa at Sunshine Senior Living. It sounds like their patience was already running thin. I've heard my parents whispering about how he didn't like it there, how he didn't follow the rules. I have no idea what rules they have, but probably ending up under arrest in Atlantic City is breaking one of them.

"You ready for school?" she asks in a trying-to-be-cheery voice. "I'm off to Maison."

My mom works at A La Maison: Home and Kitchen. She just calls it Maison, like it's a good friend. We only live a few blocks from my school, but when my mom works the early

shift I let her drive me. I think she feels guilty about leaving me to walk by myself. She's afraid I'll feel abandoned. Or maybe she thinks I'll get distracted and forget to go to school at all, which is totally possible.

So today she drops me off and calls, "Have a good day!" and as soon as she drives away I try to decide where to go that isn't a hangout spot for Charlie Kastner or his buddies. The front steps are out, and the back steps, and the hallways, because you never know where those guys are going to turn up. But then I remember that the running meeting is this afternoon and I decide to go take a look at the new track.

I cross the empty practice field and look down at an area that was filled with tractors and backhoes and cement mixers all summer. What used to be blacktop with weeds pushing up through the cracks is now a brand-new oval-shaped track, with thick green grass in the middle. The track is a bright tomato red, divided into lanes by lines painted in crisp white paint. It's all so sharp and clear, it could be in a Pixar movie. There are smaller lines painted crosswise, too, and numbers and little triangles are sprinkled around like some secret code or ancient cave writing. I want to see it up close. I want to race right down and try it out.

But I'm stopped cold at the top of the stairs. They're the same old tippy, uneven stairs that have been here since cement was invented. I hate them. They smile up at me like an ogre with cracked, crooked teeth. Forget running: these stairs are going to knock me down and chew me up before I've even made it to the organizational meeting.

I almost turn back, but I try to think of Mrs. T's saying, "Don't say 'can't.'" It's an annoying saying, because sometimes I really can't, but this time, maybe I can. I grip the metal railing and lower myself down one step at a time. Just one at a time. And despite the ogre's best attempts to pull me down, I somehow make it in one piece.

Surrounding the track is a waist-high chain-link fence. It's unlocked, so I open the gate and step in. The track smells just like it looks, all rubbery and new. Its surface makes me think of the sponge painting we did in second-grade art. I almost expect it to squish and ooze red when I press down. I wonder if Mrs. T knows all this—I bet she does.

I lift my heels and bob up and down, then I bend my knees and lay my hands flat, to get a better feel. I always like to know how things feel. There's even a name for it. Mrs. T says I'm a "tactile" learner.

I hear a voice. A girl's voice. When I look up, I see it's the new girl from PE.

"Friedman, right?" she says.

"Um . . ." I say.

"It's a pretty simple question. You are Friedman, right?"

"Yes." I don't like being called Friedman. Any sentence

that starts with "Friedman" usually ends with an order or hysterical laughter.

I stand up and brush my hands off on my pants.

"What were you doing?"

"Trying out the track."

"You're supposed to run on it, not do handstands," she says, not in an un-nice way, but maybe she's just warming up.

"I wanted to see how it felt," I say.

"You joining the track team?"

"I don't know. Are you?"

"I might."

"Aren't you playing soccer?" I ask. She looks annoyed. I feel like I've said the wrong thing. I hope she doesn't beat me up.

"I don't really like soccer. I went to soccer camp last year. The girls get mean and then they end up hating you."

Just for a second, she looks different. A little sad. I think about what my mother said, how it can't be easy for her, being better than the boys. And a ton better than the other girls. I wonder if you can be as miserable being good at something as you can being bad at it. Maybe things are reversed somehow, when you're a girl.

"Do you have a first name?" she asks me.

"Joseph."

I forget to ask hers, but she tells me anyway. "I'm Heather," she says. "We just moved here."

"Where from?"

"A place called Cherryfield, Maine," she says.

"That must be pretty different from New York."

She nods. "It's the blueberry capital of the world."

"Wow," I say.

"Aren't you going to ask?"

"Ask what?"

"Why it's called Cherryfield and not Blueberryfield?"

"Should I?"

"No," she says. "Not really. It's just that everybody does." She reaches down to touch her toes.

"I'm allergic to blueberries," I tell her. "I get itchy, way back in my throat." I demonstrate my scratching technique by sticking my finger in my ear, wiggling it around, and making a clucking sound with the back of my tongue. This is probably not something you should do on first meeting. "So, why is it?" I ask her.

"Why is what?"

"Why is it called Cherryfield if it's the blueberry capital of the world?"

"Oh. Because there used to be cherries. Before the blueberries." Then she says, "You want to run?"

"Run?"

She moves her arms and legs in a running motion. "Run. On the track. Now."

"I'm slow," I say.

"After gym class, I'm not expecting Usain Bolt."

"Who?" I ask, but she's already off, bounding along like there's nothing to it.

She's a quarter of the way around the oval before I even start running. When I finally get going, I'm surprised by how the track feels hard and soft at the same time, kind of cushiony. It makes me try tiny steps and then bigger steps and even a jump. Then I try zigzagging across the lines, out and back, holding my arms out to feel the air go by.

Heather is running straight and fast and she doesn't even slow down when she goes around the curve. She makes it look fun and easy, so I take the middle lane and try running the same way. There's something about the painted lines, all clean and sharp, that dares me to go faster, and I speed up, for about ten seconds, until I'm out of breath and have to stop.

Heather comes around and passes me, but then she stops for a second to look at something in the grassy field in the middle of the track. It's a cement circle about the size of a kiddie pool. I walk over to where she's standing and she says, "That's the discus ring." She points to the other side of the field. "Shot put's over there."

"Oh," I squeak out. That's about all the breath that's in there.

"I'm doing shot put in winter, and in spring I'll do discus, like Stephanie Brown Trafton."

"Who?"

"Stephanie Brown Trafton. She won the gold medal for discus throw in the 2008 Olympics."

I'm about to say, "Really?" but then I think it must be a trap. I know from experience that kids say things that sound logical, and then I go, "Really?" and then they laugh their heads off, because it's not true at all. Now that I think about it, she might have made up the whole Cherryfield thing, too. So, even though I'm out of breath, and light-headed and shaky, this time I see it coming. I've never even heard of this Stephanie Whoever-Whoever. I put on a "Yeah, sure" kind of voice and say, "If she really won a gold medal, I bet I would've heard of her."

"Yeah?" says Heather, and she takes a step toward me. "Well, maybe nobody's heard of her because she's not what people want to see. She's six foot four and two hundred something pounds and she throws things farther than most guys. Everybody wants to cheer for little gymnasts and pretty volleyball players in bikinis. Maybe that's why nobody's heard of her, even though she won an Olympic gold."

Heather is now about five foot ten of angriness, but she's blinking her eyes in a way that reminds me of me, when I'm trying not to cry. I want to tell her I'm sorry, that I didn't mean to hurt her feelings. I just thought she was trying to make me look stupid, like everybody else. But I don't have a chance. She shakes her head and starts to run again, much faster than I can go. At the end of the track, she crashes through the chain link gate and takes the cracked stairs back up, two at a time, and she's gone.

CHAPTER 5

SO THIS GIRL NAMED HEATHER JUST GOT HERE and yesterday she saved my life, and I've already made her hate me.

I take my seat in Social Studies and try to pay attention to Mr. Hernandez, who's telling everyone to settle down and listen, but I keep thinking about Heather. I wonder what it takes to make someone un-mad at you. Maybe if I don't say anything else stupid she'll give me another chance.

It's not like it's the first time something like this has happened. I seem to have a talent for doing exactly the wrong thing, especially where girls are concerned. There was this time in third grade, when a girl named Mary Liz sat next to me. Mary Liz was good at everything. Our teacher would always hold up her paper and say, "Look how neat Mary Liz's paper looks." Mary Liz always raised her hand at the right time. She never spoke out of turn. She never, ever had to erase so much that she went through the paper and saw the shiny, pretend-wood desk peeking through.

One day, Mrs. Jaworski told us we were going to start

learning cursive writing, even though Lee Han raised his hand and said, "My cousin says they don't even do script anymore at his school."

"Well, you're here at this school, aren't you?" said Mrs. Jaworski. "And we choose to teach cursive." Then she gave him one of those teacher stares that don't leave you any choice but to give up. I didn't even know that "cursive" meant script, so I was behind before we even started.

I sat next to Mary Liz. She was watching carefully as Mrs. Jaworski demonstrated cursive writing on the Smart Board.

"In cursive writing," said Mrs. Jaworski, "we slant our letters to the right, all at the same angle. Your letters should look like flowers, leaning toward the sun."

We all started writing and I tried, I really did. But my letters looked like somebody had stomped in the flower bed wearing army boots and left a bunch of broken stems and squashed petals.

Mrs. Jaworski walked around, looking over our shoulders. Every now and then she would pick up somebody's paper and hold it up. Of course, she held up Mary Liz's.

"Now, everyone, look how well Mary Liz is writing. Beautiful, Mary Liz." Mary Liz didn't smile. She just looked like she wanted Mrs. Jaworski to put the paper back down so she could write more beautiful words.

Mary Liz went back to work, and I couldn't help watching

her. The pencil she wrote with was longer than mine. It'd probably only been sharpened once in its whole life. She gripped it tight, looping and twirling, forming those perfect words, all lined up in pretty rows. She had nail polish that was this pearly blue-green, just a little spot of it at the end of each finger. Every few words she lifted the pencil to look at her paper. A few times, she tucked a strand of hair behind her ear before she got back to work, writing little flowers leaning toward the sun.

"Joseph," called out Mrs. Jaworski. "Are you writing or daydreaming?"

"He's staring," said Adele Sapperstein.

"Oh?" asked Mrs. Jaworski. "And what is it that's so interesting, Joseph?"

Teachers ask me that all the time. Sometimes I actually have an answer, but they never give me time to tell them, because they don't really want to know.

Adele answered for me. "He's staring at Mary Liz."

"Really," said Mrs. Jaworski. "Well, maybe if you spent less time staring at Mary Liz and more time concentrating on your writing, your paper would look better than this." She picked up my paper and held it up for the class to see.

Everybody was laughing, at my paper and at me, and somebody said, "Joseph loves Mary Liz," and then everyone laughed harder.

And that's when Mary Liz looked like the most horrifying thing that could ever happen was happening to her. She looked at me and she was mad. She was so mad at me. Sometimes I think maybe I'm why she moved away, she looked so mad.

I took my paper and crumpled it up and threw it on the floor. Mrs. Jaworski got angry with me, which didn't make any sense at all, since she was the one who'd said it was terrible.

I ended up out in the hall, which was not that unusual, but mostly I remember that day because of how Mary Liz looked at me.

And now I've done it again.

I hear the sound of chairs scraping the floor, and everyone in my Social Studies class is gathering their stuff and going to the door.

"Where are we going?" I ask nobody in particular.

"To the library," says a girl named Carly. "Don't you ever listen?"

I don't even bother answering that. I just pick up my backpack and follow the others to the library.

CHAPTER 6

OUR LIBRARIAN IS MRS. FISHBEIN. SHE HAS WHITE hair and always wears skirts. There's a rumor that she lives here in the library, eating nothing but Cup O' Noodles. She has dozens of them stacked on shelves over her desk. I happen to know the rumor isn't true, because sometimes I ride my bicycle through the school parking lot after all the cars are gone, and I see her leaving and walking toward the bus stop. I haven't told anybody, mostly because I don't know who I would tell and also because it's nobody's business.

There are odd things about Mrs. Fishbein, though. For one thing, her office is filled with piles of yellow cards. They're there because she doesn't like computers. She told us that when they first delivered the computer system, they had to take away the card catalogue cabinets. She gave them up "kicking and screaming." Those were the words she used, "kicking and screaming." She made them take out every last catalogue card and pile them in her office. Every single one.

She also kept the stampers and stamp pads, and the

green cards for signing books out. What if there's a disaster and we're all plunged back into the Stone Age, she once explained. Then who'll be laughing: the whole world with their empty screens and dead keyboards, or her, safe in the library, with books you can hold in your hand, catalogue cards to find them with, and lined green cards for signing them out?

The thing is, if the world is in ruins, I wonder if we're really going to be worrying about sign-outs and returns.

Anyway, when we get to the library, the chairs are set up in a horseshoe. It reminds me of third-grade story time, but in seventh grade nobody reads you stories.

I take a seat in one of the chairs. They're the gray, slippery kind. The kind your rear just can't get a good grip on. I feel myself sliding and do my best to hold on.

Once we're all sitting down, Mrs. Fishbein says, "As Mr. Hernandez explained, each of you will be researching a topic of your choice." It's news to me. "And even though there is a lot of information online, there is still value in doing some of your research in the library."

I see Jessica Yu roll her eyes and Jordan Glazer stifle a laugh.

"And in the library," Mrs. Fishbein continues, "even if computers have replaced the card catalogue, you still need to find books on the shelves. And that's where the Dewey Decimal system comes in."

The class collapses in moans and groans, but Mrs. Fishbein bravely carries on. "In 1876 . . ."

"Eighteen seventy-six?" whines Jordan Glazer. "Seriously?"

". . . Melvil Dewey invented our system to organize books. . ."

Oddly enough, while the other kids find this Dewey Decimal thing hilarious or boring or hilariously boring, I think it's kind of fascinating. Once you get past "F" for Fiction and "B" for Biography, books are organized with numbers, down to the last little detail. Science is in the 500s, animals are 590s, mammals are 599, and camels, deer, giraffes, and hippos have a number that's just theirs: 599.73.

I start wondering where I'd find toilet paper or peanut butter or killer bees. I try to figure out what number I'd have— if I'd be in the 900s for being from New York, the 400s for speaking English, the 500s for being a primate, or back in the 100s for going to the school psychologist. I wonder who decides which part of you is the most important, and if they're always right.

I picture myself scattered all around the library, a little bit of me here, a little bit there.

The problem is, while I'm thinking about that, Mrs. Fishbein is explaining the exercise we're about to do. That's when the other kids somehow know to start listening. And that's the part I always miss.

So I'm not expecting it when Nicole Abruzzi sticks a pencil in my face, point first, just as I'm reaching for a worksheet that Patrick McCarthy is holding just out of my reach, so I just miss getting my eye poked out. Then Mrs. Fishbein plops a book in my lap. It's called *Get in Shape, Boys! A Teen Guide to Getting Strong, Being Fit, and Feeling Confident.* It's got pictures of all these buff-looking guys on the cover. One has his shirt open with all these muscles popping out, and two have pretty girlfriends smiling up at them.

The exercise has something to do with the book's Dewey Decimal number, but I'm not sure what. I have the pencil in one hand and the paper in the other, and this big, heavy book in my lap.

Everybody around me is looking inside their book, scribbling away on their worksheet, and filling in the blanks, but I have three objects and two hands and I don't have a clue what the assignment is. So I do what I do sometimes. I just sit there, wondering how everyone else doesn't seem to have a problem, when I do.

There's always someone who calls attention to this habit of mine, and now it's Nicole Abruzzi, who has her own habit of pulling down her stretchy top. She does that now and says, "Joseph is just sitting there." Then everyone looks at me and at the book in my lap, and everybody laughs. And I swear, I'm not even moving, but somehow that's when my rear loses its grip on the slippery gray chair and I land on the floor.

I'm expecting Mrs. Fishbein to be mad because I wasn't listening and because I'm on the floor, but instead she gives the class a sharp, warning look. They stop laughing. Out loud, anyway. She takes the pencil out of my right hand and takes the work sheet out of my left hand and heaves *Get in Shape, Boys! A Teen Guide to Getting Strong, Being Fit, and Feeling Confident* off my lap. Somehow she still has a hand left. She gently holds my wrist and leads me over to a table.

Then she tells me what I have to do. The point is to write on the work sheet all the information about *Get in Shape, Boys! A Teen Guide to Getting Strong, Being Fit, and Feeling Confident* I would need if I had to find the book and use it in a research paper: the title, the author, the publisher, when and where it was published, and, of course, the Dewey Decimal number.

She asks if I have any questions, and I don't. Sitting at the table makes it much easier than having it all in my lap. If Mrs. T was here, she'd know that the spaces on the worksheet are way too small for my handwriting, especially with the title *Get in Shape, Boys! A Teen Guide to Getting Strong, Being Fit, and Feeling Confident*, and she'd give me a separate sheet of paper to write my answers on. But I do what I can, making a sharp right turn at the edge of the paper, writing down the side, and squashing it in at the bottom of the page.

When the bell rings, Mrs. Fishbein tells the class to leave their books, worksheets, and pencils on their chairs, and they're all out in the hall in about three seconds. I, on the other hand, watch my work sheet catch the breeze from the closing door and float away, while my pencil rolls off the table in the other direction.

Mrs. Fishbein starts collecting the other kids' work sheets. I'm reaching under a table to retrieve mine when I hear her say with a chuckle, "Maybe it is time for me to retire."

"I'm sorry," I say. "Am I that bad?"

"Oh, Joseph, not you!" says Mrs. Fishbein. She sits down on one of those slippery chairs and pats the one beside her. "I just mean, after all these years, I still make so many mistakes. I didn't mean to make the morning a bad one for you."

I hand her my work sheet, which has handwriting going in about six different directions. I sit down next to her, holding on this time, so I don't slide too far. "It's okay," I say. "It wasn't really any worse than usual."

"They offered me a nice retirement package," she says. "But I didn't feel ready." Sometimes adults talk to me like I'm one of them. It's kind of like when a funny-colored duck is rejected by its flock, and a kindly goose takes it in. "I didn't feel finished yet. With what, I'm not sure. But I've always felt that there are possibilities in everything, if you don't give up." She glances at my work sheet and she doesn't even look disappointed. Then she looks back at me. "But maybe I'm just old and outdated, like poor Melvil Dewey."

I'm about to tell her how much I like the Dewey Decimal system, but then the bell rings and she looks at the clock. "Oh, my!" she says, popping up. "Now I've made you late. Let me get you a late pass."

As she's writing out a pass, I keep thinking about *Get in Shape, Boys! A Teen Guide to Getting Strong, Being Fit, and Feeling Confident*. I can feel those guys looking over at me, daring me to join them in their smiling, muscled confidence.

"Um, Mrs. Fishbein?" I say.

"Yes, Joseph."

"Can I um . . . borrow that book?"

Her face lights up. "Of course! Of course you can! Bring it over here." I go get it and plunk it on the desk and she takes the bar-code reader from its cradle. She wrinkles her nose at it. "Let's see if this thing works. It was on the fritz yesterday . . ."

She points the little red laser line at the book and flinches when it goes *blip*. I put the book in my backpack so no one can see it.

Mrs. Fishbein hands me my late pass. "Have a good day, Joseph," she says.

"Thanks," I say. "And, Mrs. Fishbein?"

"Yes, Joseph?"

"You shouldn't retire. You're a really good librarian and I like the Dewey Decimal system."

Mrs. Fishbein smiles at me. "Thank you, Joseph. Me, too."

I step out into the hall, my backpack now three times heavier. It's only the second day of school, and I realize my next class is a total mystery to me.

Instead of finding my schedule, I take a guess that it's English, and since I'm late, the door is closed. When I open it, I'm staring at a bunch of eighth-graders who take one look at my shocked face and burst out laughing. I have to wonder, *Don't any of them ever make a mistake? Doesn't anybody know what it feels like?*

I guess not, because even after the door closes behind me, I can hear the teacher banging on the desk to get their attention. In the hallway, I dig into my backpack and find my schedule, crumpled and squashed at the bottom. My next class is French. I hurry through the halls, but by the time I get there, class has already started. Madame Labelle is rattling happily away in a language I can't even hope to understand.

CHAPTER 7

I TRY TO BE QUIET AND NOT INTERRUPT MADAME Labelle, so I put the late pass on her desk and slide into the first chair I see. It's only after I sit down that I see Heather is next to me. I didn't even know she was in my French class. She gives me a quick glance, but she's paying attention to Madame Labelle. I think she's still mad. But then I think, *Maybe she's not mad, maybe she's just a good student.*

Madame Labelle is speaking in French. She told us yesterday that the best way to learn a language is to hear it spoken, but that seems backward to me. It would make more sense for the learning part to come first. I admit, it sounds nice—kind of singsong, like the way you talk to a pet—but I doubt I'll ever catch on to what any of it means.

Heather is still paying attention, but every few seconds she looks down at her desk. I see that she's drawing something. It's in pencil. I watch her scritch and scratch on the pad, but I can't make out what she's sketching.

Madame Labelle is tall and thin and she's wearing a short, sleeveless dress, so you can see how muscly her arms and legs

are. She has on green high heels, and they click on the check-ered tan-and-brown tile. She does this thing where after ev-ery sentence she turns on one pointy heel and clicks off in a completely new direction. Usually she turns on a brown tile, but sometimes on a tan one. She clicks to the left. She clicks to the right.

When she starts clicking my way, I realize I'm in trouble.

Madame Labelle is looking at me and she's waiting for me to say something. After a few seconds, she taps her ear and says a word that sounds like *Ay cootay* and then she turns to a boy named Gregory, who says something like "Germ lapel Gregory."

Then she turns to Heather, who is hiding her notepad on her lap, under the desk. Heather says, "Germ lapel Heather."

So then Madame Labelle looks back at me and even I can figure out what I'm supposed to do. "Germ lapel Joseph," I say. Madame Labelle gives me one of those warning smiles that aren't really smiles at all, and clicks off to the front of the room, where she turns her back to us and starts to write on the whiteboard.

I start to copy what she's writing, but it's hard when the letters seem randomly lined up and apostrophes are flying all over the place. Then I hear a thunk and I look down to see that Heather's notepad has slid off her lap. It lands in the aisle between us. Madame Labelle hardly even glances over her shoulder. Since it's coming from my general direction, she probably assumes it's just me being my usual clumsy self.

When I lean over to pick up the notepad, I see what Heather's been drawing. It's Madame Labelle, but she's a frog, with long muscly legs and high heels. I try not to laugh as I hand it back to Heather. She takes it without looking at me, puts it back on her lap, and gets back to copying down what Madame Labelle is writing: *"Je m'appelle . . ."* and then, *"Comment t'appelles-tu?"* I copy it as well as I can. My mom took French, and she works at Maison, which is a French name, so I figure I can ask her what it means later.

The rest of the period goes by in a blur of gargled "r"s and puckered "ooh"s, and when the bell rings, I run after Heather.

"Heather, wait up," I call out, trying to sound like we're old friends.

She stops and turns.

"You draw really well," I add.

Heather shrugs. "I got in the habit at my old school," she explains, "when I got bored in class."

"Yeah, I know what you mean," I say, even though boredom isn't really my main problem. "You should draw Mr. Tompkins. The principal. He looks like a walrus."

"He might be more manatee than walrus," she says. "You can't jump to conclusions. You have to study someone to know for sure."

As she's talking, I feel like she's studying me that way. I wonder if she notices how my backpack is riding low on my back, weighted down with *Get in Shape, Boys!* Or how my sweatshirt doesn't have buttons or a zipper, because I only wear buttons or a zipper if I absolutely have to. I wonder what animal she'd draw me as. After this morning, probably some annoying insect or a monkey. I hope I'm not a monkey.

Maybe it's not too late to change her mind. "I'm sorry about before," I say. "About not believing you. I bet she's a really good athlete. That girl you told me about. I mean, she'd have to be, right? If she won a medal?"

"A gold medal," she says.

"Right," I say. "I thought you were tricking me. A lot of people do that here."

"That's mean," she says. "To trick somebody."

"That's why they do it," I say.

She's studying me even harder now. She stares at me for what seems like a whole minute, then she gets a kind of half smile on her face, like she's made up her mind. Like she's decided that I'm some kind of furry, harmless creature. A gerbil, maybe. Or a hamster.

"We had a walrus type in Cherryfield," she says. "Mr. Sammell. I drew every teacher like ten times. Cherryfield is pretty small."

"Smaller than Lakeview?"

"Way smaller. My mom grew up there. She was Blueberry Princess three years in a row." I can't tell if she's proud of that or not. It sounds more like one of those things you've heard your parents say a million times and now it's just annoying.

"There isn't an anything princess here, is there?" she asks me.

"No."

"And Lakeview isn't the anything capital of the world?"

"I don't think so."

She nods. Then she says, "So, you going to the track meeting later?"

"Um, yeah. Sure," I answer, trying to sound like it was never in doubt.

"Okay. See you there," she says, starting down the hallway.

"Wait," I call after her. "What was her name again? The Olympics person?"

"Stephanie Brown Trafton," she calls back, "Beijing 2008 Summer Olympics, gold medal in discus, two hundred and twelve feet, five inches." Then she breaks into a trot, and just like on the track this morning, she's gone.

CHAPTER 8

AFTER SCHOOL, AS I'M GATHERING MY STUFF AT my locker, I realize that Grandpa is probably home. I really want to hear about how prison was in Atlantic City, but now I've promised Mrs. T and Heather that I'll go to the track meeting. There's no way I'm going to disappoint them both, so I go to Room D-5. There's a sign on the door:

Track/Cross Country Meeting:
Lower Field Track

I run down the hall, out the back door, and across the upper field. It's not a good sign that I'm already out of breath. When I reach the old concrete stairs, I use this morning's technique. I grab the railing and wobble down to the track, where a group of kids is waiting.

There are four boys and five girls. I know their names, but the only ones I've ever spoken to are Sanjit and Erica from the Resource Room. And Heather. Three of the boys are standing around whacking the ground with their heels, and the girls

are comparing shoelaces. Except for Heather. She's standing on the outside of the crowd.

"I'm late," I tell her. I'm not quite sure why. It's not like she's in charge.

"Coach isn't here yet," she says with a shrug. I like the way she says "Coach," like she's done this before. Like she's called somebody "Coach" and knows what it feels like.

"Do you know who it is?" asks a kid named Sammy Small. He is, as a matter of fact, small, and he's hanging from a branch of a big maple tree, trying to shake the leaves off. Sammy seems to have a little bit of an energy problem. I wonder if he should be in the Resource Room.

"Who who is?" answers Heather.

"The coach."

"No," she says, and Sammy drops down and runs back to the boys' group.

"I bet it's DeSalvo," says a boy named Wes. He has a lot of curly hair that droops down just below his eyebrows.

"No way. DeSalvo does soccer," Sammy says.

"O'Mara?"

"Nah. He's girls' tennis," says Sanjit.

"Ugh, don't mention girls' tennis," says a girl named Victoria. She's standing with her friend Teresa, which is not surprising. They've been inseparable since elementary school. I remember seeing them practice cartwheels at recess, and sometimes I hear them talking to each other in Spanish.

"Why?" asks Sanjit.

"We joined the rec squad last year," says Teresa. "We were on the bench the entire time."

"If you haven't taken lessons since you were, like, four, forget it," adds Victoria.

"I got cut from travel soccer three years in a row," says a girl named Brianne.

"Little League," says a kid named Mark, "I got bumped down to the minors."

I'm starting to see a pattern here.

"I wonder if there are cuts in track," says Sanjit.

"I don't know, but my older brother says in high school they make you run till you throw up," says Wes.

"Sweet," says Sammy.

I hear a grinding sound coming from the direction of the gym. It reminds me of the noise a garbage truck makes when it chews up trash. When I look over, I see that it's Mr. Papasian clearing his throat. For one horrible second, I think maybe he's our coach, but then I see the football players behind him.

"Let's go, gentlemen," he's saying in his scratchy voice. "Get your lazy a—" Then there's a pause. "We're not out here to admire nature's bounty."

"Nature's what?" says Sammy.

"Bounty," Teresa says. "Leaves and stuff."

"He has to watch how he talks," explains Wes. "He had to go to anger management, so he can't yell or use bad language."

"I heard he threw a brick at a kid," says Brianne.

"It was just a Lego. My sister was there," says Victoria.

As they discuss Coach Papasian, I see what's slowing the football players down. Charlie Kastner and Zachary are having a spitting contest. It seems like Zachary is winning the contest, but then Charlie stops mid spit-launch when he sees something way more entertaining: us.

His eyes get big and he starts to smile, looking us over like we're a box of doughnuts he just opened and every single one is frosted or cream-filled.

"Look!" calls Charlie. "Look. Are they . . . some kind of team?" Zachary shrugs. "Friedman! Are you joining a girls' team or something? What sport is it, Friedman? Knitting?"

I don't say anything, but Wes calls back, "It's track, you moron. And it's not a girls' team."

The "moron" part doesn't even seem to register with Charlie. Maybe that's because now his eyes are fixed on Heather. "Hey, he's right!" he calls out merrily. "It's not a girls' team. Look who's on it." He points at Heather. She's ignoring him, leaning on a big tree and stretching one leg out behind her. A few of Charlie's other football friends have gathered around now and they're laughing.

"Hey you! Miss Hip Check! Come over here. We need a right tackle!"

"Kastner!" calls out Coach Papasian. "Mind your own business."

"It is my business, Coach," says Charlie. "I'm recruiting for the football team."

"Yeah, Coach, look at her. She could play linebacker!" says Zachary.

"Yeah, linebacker," calls Charlie. "Or tackle. So what do you say?"

Heather stays perfectly calm. "I could," she says, straightening up and staring back at Charlie, "except that I don't like football. And besides, I've got a team."

It dawns on me that she means us.

"Kastner!" calls out Coach Papasian. "One lap around the field!" At first, I think he's punishing Charlie for tormenting us, but then he clarifies. "You're holding up practice."

"Okay, okay," says Charlie. But before he goes, he calls out to Heather, "Say hi to your dad for me." It sounds like a taunt, but I don't know why.

Heather blinks, but she doesn't say anything back. She just goes back to the tree and starts stretching again.

The rest of us try to pretend nothing much happened. Heather is bending over, holding her ankles in a stretch. I go over nearby and try to reach mine, but I don't get very far, barely past my knees.

"He knows your dad?" I ask, hanging upside down.

"Cloverdale," she answers. Cloverdale is a golf club on the other side of town.

"You belong there?"

Heather lets out a noisy puff of air. "No. Charlie does. My dad works there."

"Does he teach golf?" I ask. The blood is rushing to my head. I'm getting dizzy.

"No, he's a horticulturist." I guess even the fact that my cheeks are falling into my eyes doesn't disguise the blank expression on my face. "He's a plant expert," she explains, "and a master gardener."

I don't want to seem uninterested, but another minute of this and I might pass out. "How long are you going to stay upside down?" I ask. Heather touches her toes and straightens up, so I do, too. I think she wants to laugh at me, but she doesn't. I appreciate that. Once my head stops spinning, I say, "So Cloverdale needs a plant expert?"

"Are you kidding?" she says. "When we got here my dad found Pythium blight and basal rot in the turf, and slime mold all over the place." This really doesn't help my queasiness. "And bronze birch borer beetles in the trees."

"Bronze birch . . ."

"Borer beetles. They're really hard to get rid of."

"But your dad knows how?"

"Well, yeah," she says, like it's a no-brainer. "He has a degree from the University of Maine."

Just then, one of the girls calls out, "Look! I think it's our coach."

We both look in the direction she's pointing. A figure is coming down the stairs. It's hard to make out, because the sun is in our eyes, but it's someone wearing sweats and sneakers. I'm not positive, but I think it's a she. As the figure gets closer, I blink and blink because I'm sure I'm making it up. But when I look at Sanjit, he has the same unbelieving look, and Erica does, too.

"Isn't that the Resource Room lady?" says Brianne.

"Holy moly," says Sanjit.

And I realize that there, dressed in sweatpants and a sweatshirt, wearing bright white sneakers with pink laces and green soles, is our track coach: Mrs. T.

CHAPTER 9

I'M STARING AT THOSE PINK-LACED SNEAKERS and trying to wrap my head around Mrs. T being the coach. In a way, it makes sense. She's practically a coach in the Resource Room, cheering us all on, coaxing us to do better. But she didn't give any clue when she read the announcement that day, and it's not like her to keep secrets. She's never mentioned being an athlete or even liking sports. And it just doesn't quite compute, seeing her like this—out in the wild, in sweats, with a whistle around her neck.

"So," she says, looking at all our confused faces, "I hope you're ready to run."

"Wait, where's our coach?" asks Wes.

Mrs. T points to herself and smiles.

"I mean the boys' coach."

She looks over her shoulder and then points to herself again.

"So, boys and girls are on the same team?" Teresa asks. She gives a sideways look at Sammy Small, who started running in place as soon as Mrs. T said "ready to run."

"In cross country we train together," answers Mrs. T. "In most races you'll run separately, but we're all one big cozy team."

"What's cross country?" asks Mark. "I thought this was track."

"There are three seasons," explains Mrs. T, holding up three long fingers. "In the fall, we do cross country. In the winter, there's track and field. You can do sprints, hurdles, distance running, or field events like long jump, high jump, and shot put."

"Here?" asks Sanjit, looking confused. "In winter? What if it snows?"

"Don't worry, Sanjit," says Mrs. T, smiling. "We use an indoor track at the community college. In spring, we're back here, outside, and we add even more events, like discus, and maybe even javelin."

When she mentions discus I look at Heather, giving her what I mean to be a friendly, approving, and slightly apologetic smile. I have a feeling it comes out more like a dorky, I-have-to-go-to-the-bathroom face.

"But what do you do in cross country?" asks Victoria.

"We run!" says Mrs. T. "We run a course of about one and a half miles."

"One and a half miles?" says Wes.

"Is she crazy?" mutters Teresa.

"*Loca*," Victoria says with a nod.

"And the fun part is, we'll have meets at different schools, and no two courses are the same."

Brianne slowly raises her hand. "What's a meet?"

"It's a race," answers Mrs. T. "I guess it's called that because it's where teams 'meet' to race. Good point, Brianne!" Brianne looks surprised that she made any point at all. "So!" Mrs. T claps her hands together. "I've mapped out our home course: twice around, starting by the field, going into the woods, up White Oak Lane, around the gym, and back. You're going to love it!"

None of us looks so sure.

"Now, since this is a pilot program—"

"Zzzzrooom," goes Sammy. "Eh-eh-eh-eh." He's pretending to be a fighter pilot.

"Thank you, Sammy. 'Pilot' as in brand-new." She starts again. "Because this is a pilot program, we'll be learning as we go. But the most exciting thing," says Mrs. T, as if what she already said was exciting enough, "is that we get to hold the last meet, the league championship, here at Lakeview!" She holds both hands to her head, like it's about to explode, this is so exciting. "So, any more questions?"

"Are there cuts?" asks Sanjit.

"Cuts?" Mrs. T looks confused.

"If we don't run fast enough, do we get cut from the team?"

Erica explains. She hasn't said much, but I guess she was listening all along.

"All I ask is that you do your best. As long as you're trying, you are a part of this team."

Victoria and Teresa give each other a soft high five.

"Are there trophies?" Wes asks.

"Some meets will give trophies to the top finishers; sometimes the top teams get medals. But what cross country is about, what I want you to strive for, every race, is a PR."

"A what?" asks Sanjit.

"A personal record. Some people call it a personal best, but I like the sound of 'PR.' It means, whatever you run today, you're trying to do better tomorrow. You're trying to do your best. Not anybody else's, just yours."

"As long as there are trophies," mutters Wes.

Mrs. T tells us some things about schedules and attendance and days off, but it pretty much gets by me. I'm still going over that PR idea. It sounds like good news. Beating myself has to be a lot easier than trying to beat anybody else.

"Do we get uniforms?" Sammy asks. I don't think he's really been listening, either. He probably does belong in the Resource Room.

"Yes, Sammy, but we're just getting started. You have to earn them. Now is everybody ready for a warm-up?" There's not a peep. "Of course you are! We'll start with two laps."

Brianne starts to raise her hand, but before she even asks, Mrs. T explains, "One lap is once around the track. So, we're going twice around. Okay? Let's go!"

There are a few seconds when we all just stand there, but then Heather starts out. The other girls follow her and then Sammy sprints out to catch them.

"Slow down!" calls Mrs. T. "Everybody, slow down! We're warming up!" But nobody is listening. Wes and Mark scramble out behind Sammy, and the three of them race to pass the four girls. Sanjit and I bring up the rear.

At first, I'm just enjoying the day. I look up at the sky. It looks bluer than ever next to the dark green of the maples. The air smells all sugary from the fresh mowed grass. Up ahead, a robin darts away when he sees me coming. The sun is shining like it's still a summer afternoon, and the track feels warm, like it's been soaking up heat for days and days just so it could push it back up to me. I like the idea that the track is here especially for this. It isn't like running on a street, or running because you're late, or running away. It's running, just to run.

I look down at the red, rubbery track and watch my feet flying along, left, right, left, right, even around the turns. The others are ahead of me, so I go faster, trying to catch up. It feels great, I feel fast and free . . . until I start to feel a little pain in my side. At first it's like somebody's pinching me near my ribs, and I can ignore it. But then it grows into a pain like somebody's stabbing me with a butcher's knife.

I look around and see that everybody else is slowing down, too. A couple of the girls hold their sides, like they have the same pain, and then I almost trip over Sammy Small, who's sitting in the middle lane, trying to catch his breath and rubbing his ribs the same way. I wonder if it's possible that we all got appendicitis at the same time.

By the time I hear Mrs. T's whistle, we're strewn around the track on our backs, sides, and faces, like a bunch of dead flies after a lethal dose of Raid. Except for Heather. She has her fingers laced together and her arms up high over her head and she's bending side to side, looking like everything feels just great. In a few seconds I see a pair of white sneakers with pink laces and green soles next to me.

I look up at Mrs. T. "Did I do something to make you want to kill me?" I ask.

"It's just a cramp," she says. "Sometimes it's called a stitch. You all went out way too fast. You'll learn to pace yourself."

"Why didn't you tell us you were the coach?"

Mrs. T puts her hand on her head, just like she does in the Resource Room. "I didn't want you to do it for me. I wanted you to do it for yourself," she says. Then she calls out, "Okay! Good start, everybody!"

Looking around at the bodies sprawled around the track, I wonder what a bad start would be.

"Everybody up. Let's walk a lap and then one more time around."

My side still hurts, but I peel myself from the track and start to walk next to Mark. He doesn't look much better than I do.

Heather looks like she could happily run ten more laps. I think she's going to give me some words of encouragement as she passes by, but instead she says, "Go home and have a banana."

I assume that's some kind of put-down. You'd think I'd know them all by now, but there are always new ones.

I finish walking my lap and then limp around one more time. By the time I get back over to Mrs. T, she's handing out cards that say "Emergency Contacts" on top. I only hope I can finish filling it in before I become an emergency.

The other kids fill in their blanks and crowd around Mrs. T. "Okay, great job, everybody," she says, collecting their forms. "Tomorrow we'll really get to work! Same time, same place!"

Heather shoves her form in my hand. "Give this to her, okay? I want to do a couple more while I'm still warmed up." She starts to run. Again.

I'm the last to finish my emergency form, which is no

surprise. There's nothing to write on but my knee. It looks like I've filled it in on a bumper car ride, but somehow I've managed to fit in information for CONTACT 1, my mom, and CONTACT 2, my dad. I glance at Heather's form. She's filled in: CONTACT 1: Michael Konstantinidis. If that were my name, I'd still be in first grade, trying to fit it all in a worksheet space, but she's written it perfectly straight and neat. Relationship to student: father. She's put his work number and his cell number. CONTACT 2 is blank.

As everybody gathers their stuff and heads off, I limp over toward Mrs. T. I hand her my form and Heather's. "Good job, Joseph," she says, patting me on the shoulder.

I go back to where I left my things and pick up my backpack. It feels extra heavy, and I remember that *Get in Shape, Boys!* is in there, the teens on the cover probably snickering at my condition.

Before I head home, I look over at the track. Heather is still running. Another two laps, or even three. And she's not even breathing hard.

CHAPTER 10

THERE'S GOOD NEWS WHEN I GET HOME FROM school. Grandpa's back.

He's sitting in the den, in the chair he likes best, a big leather recliner, listening to some people singing opera.

I give him a hug, and the recliner rocks us both like it's hugging us, too. "What was jail like?" I ask.

"A step up from that Sundown place, if you ask me," he says.

"Sunshine," Mom says, coming in from the kitchen. She hands him some coffee and I take a seat on the sofa. "Sunshine Senior Living."

"Everybody's over seventy-five," says Grandpa. "Trust me: it's Sundown."

"I'm just glad you're back," Mom says, "after your unfortunate night out." Grandpa looks at me and winks.

"What did you do, anyway?" I ask.

"Nothing. I did nothing that a free man in a free country shouldn't be able to do. I took a walk and went to Caesar's."

"Dad, you were with a group," Mom says. She's picking up

the dishes that Grandpa has left around the den. "You can't just walk away without telling them."

"Those people move like clams. Everybody's got a cane, or one of those strollers."

"Walkers," my mother says, with a sigh.

"It takes them half an hour just to get off the bus. Three little steps, you'd think they were coming down Mount Everest. And," he says, shaking his head, "they dropped us at some second-rate casino with nasty bar girls and stale peanuts. I like Caesar's."

My mother sighs again and adds a cereal bowl and a cup to her pile.

"Then all of a sudden the police are after me," Grandpa continues. "Like I'm Bugsy Siegel or something."

"Everyone was looking for you, Dad. They thought you were lost."

"Lost. I'm a grown man. I can take care of myself. Those Sundown people, they're a bunch of bubbies. Always nudging. 'Mr. Schatzkis, time for breakfast.' 'Mr. Schatzkis, time for lunch.'"

My mother sits down on the coffee table and speaks gently to him. "Remember, Dad, when you were on your own, last year after Mom died. You weren't eating . . ."

Grandpa waves his hand like he's brushing away a fly. "I was eating," he says. "I ate less. It's boring eating by yourself. And I was sad. Can you blame me for being sad?"

"Of course not," says Mom. She has on her trying-to-be-patient voice. "But that's why we didn't want you to be alone. You didn't want to live here with us . . ."

"I didn't want to be a burden."

"So we thought you'd be better off at Sunshine. And you agreed."

Grandpa gives a little grunt.

"It's not a nursing home, for goodness' sake," Mom goes on, "it's a beautiful senior living residence. It's got a nine-hole golf course."

"I don't play golf. And I didn't know it was run by crazy people who lock you up for taking a walk!"

"They called the police to find you," says Mom, getting up. "They were worried. And you were the one who requested the jail cell."

"I'm at the police station, I want a place to lie down," answers Grandpa.

"So you got what you asked for," Mom says, the stack of dishes rattling in her hands. "Now do us a favor and stay here with us. I work most days, and Joseph can use the company." She marches off to the kitchen. "And this time, I don't need an argument." I hear her drop the dishes into the sink with a clank.

Grandpa winces and looks at me. "She has a point about the jail cell part, but don't tell her I said so," he whispers.

The people on the radio have finished singing, and he motions for me to come over next to him. I sit on the chair's puffy arm and he ruffles my hair, which is all sweaty.

"What've you been up to? Playing ball?" he asks.

"Running," I answer. "Cross country."

"What country are you crossing?"

"None, Grandpa. It's the name of the sport. Cross country running."

"Well," he says, "are you fast?"

"No. I'm terrible. But Mrs. T says I'll get better. She's the coach, and also my Resource Room teacher."

A man on the radio is telling us what comes next, but Grandpa clicks it off with the remote. "Resource Room. That's because your attention drifts?"

"Yeah," I answer.

"Mine, too. And it's not because I'm seventy-nine. It drifted when I was forty-nine. It drifted when I was nine."

"I read really slowly."

Grandpa nods.

"And I feel stupid a lot."

"Join the club."

"Sometimes I have trouble sitting still."

"Then running sounds like a good solution, doesn't it?"

Huh. I hadn't really thought about it that way. "Did you go to the Resource Room when you were a kid?" I ask him.

"There wasn't any Resource Room. The teachers called me stupid and the other kids beat the daylights out of me. They don't do that anymore?"

"No. They make fun of me sometimes, though."

"Sticks and stones," says Grandpa.

I guess that means things are better than they used to be and I shouldn't complain.

"So, you don't want to go back to Sunshine?" I ask. I sort of hope he doesn't. I like having him to talk to. Grandpa shrugs and pushes the lever on the recliner. It makes the headrest snap into an upright position, giving the back of his head a whack and sending us both rocking.

"Sunshine," he mutters, pulling himself out of the puffy chair. "They try to tell you what to eat, how to walk, what girls to wink at. They'd tell me when to go to the bathroom if they could."

I think about all the times they do that in school. Not only the teachers, but the older kids, the cool kids, the bullies, letting you know what's okay and what's not. Maybe you never get away from them. Maybe they follow you your whole life.

Grandpa is heading for the bathroom. "They think they can make the rules about getting old?" he says. "Well, you know what I think?" He turns around and whispers, like he's sharing this secret only with me, "I think it's time to tell them all to mind their own beeswax."

CHAPTER 11

THE NEXT DAY, FOR SOME REASON EVEN I DON'T understand, I come to practice. I haven't really filled my parents in about any of this, because this might possibly be my first real practice and my last. Maybe I came because I told Grandpa. Or it could be because of Heather or Mrs. T. I also have the weird idea that it has something to do with that searing pain in my side. Not that I had it, but that everybody else had it, too. Maybe I've had enough years of personal defeat and I'm ready to give shared misery a try.

It's possible that the others feel the same way, because they're all back. This time Mrs. T is already there to greet us. I go stand with Wes and Mark. Wes is licking what looks like ketchup off his fingers. He wipes what's left on his shorts.

Teresa is watching. "Ugh," she says.

"What?" says Wes.

"Were those fries?" she asks.

"They were left over from lunch. I wasn't going to let them go to waste."

"Ugh," she says again.

"Okay," Mrs. T calls out, but Sammy raises his hand.

"Yes, Sammy?"

"Mrs. T—" he starts.

"Coach," says Mrs. T. "Call me Coach, or Coach T."

"Okay, so Mrs. . . . Coach," says Sammy, "are we getting uniforms?"

"Like I told you yesterday," she says, "you are getting uniforms. But you have to put in some work first."

"The girls like guys who have uniforms," Sammy whispers to Mark. Then he smiles and raises his eyebrows in Victoria's direction. She doesn't seem particularly charmed.

Coach T claps her hands and gathers us around. "Okay. Today we start our training."

"Oh, boy," mumbles Mark.

"Here's the plan: we'll warm up with two laps around the track. Slow and easy. Remember yesterday. When you go out too fast, you pay for it. Right, Victoria?"

"What?" says Victoria, who has been busy fastening her ponytail.

"Yesterday, everyone went out way too fast," Coach T says in a clear, loud voice, so nobody can say they didn't hear. "Today we're going to run two laps, how? Sanjit?"

"Slow and easy," Sanjit says. He really loves Mrs. T.

"That's right. Slow and easy. Then we'll take a rest and

go through the woods to White Oak Lane. Just follow the arrows, they're spray-painted on the trail. At White Oak, we'll take the hill, and I'll meet you at the top. Remember: Slow. Take walk breaks. Are we ready?"

Good thing she doesn't wait for a response.

"Let's go!"

Heather starts first, and the rest of us scurry behind her. This won't be so bad, I think. This time I'll stay relaxed. This time I'll take it slow. Slow and easy.

But I don't get past my first few steps before I see it.

Goose poop.

Piles and piles of green-brown goose poop logs, all over the start of the track. They're like big fat green worms, and they make me feel like I do around green olives, hard-boiled egg yolks, and batting eyes on a baby doll: frozen and queasy. The girls are hopscotching around it, but I can't move.

"Joseph," says Mrs. T, but I can barely hear her. Bells of goose poop panic are ringing in my ears. It's a goose poop minefield. A nightmare of goose poop.

"Just step around them. It clears up."

I want to move, I really do. Coach tries to take my hand, but I pull back. All I can think is I can't, I can't, I can't, I can't.

Out of the corner of my eye, I can see the rest of the team. They're rounding the far turn. They're already halfway around, with Heather in the lead. Soon they'll be here and they'll know what a hopeless coward I am.

I take a deep breath and stare down the little green cylinders. Maybe if I close my eyes . . . but then I might step in some. So I try squinting, which seems like a logical middle ground. I hold my breath so no stray goose poop molecules will enter my body, and I start to tiptoe.

"Go, Joseph. You can do it!" shouts Coach T—a cheer that's probably never been used for someone who's moving as slowly as I am. But I take a step and another. I'm halfway through. Up ahead the track is clear, if I can just go a few steps more. I step and step and then, when I'm almost there, where the goose poop ends and the red track is clean and clear, some flight instinct kicks in and I rocket away, into the beautiful un-goose-pooped lanes.

I can't believe it. I breathe in deep and run with my chest puffed out, basking in my own bravery. I feel like a goose poop conqueror, like I could take on an olive, or split-pea soup, or stare down that icky gray film that surrounds an egg yolk.

But then Heather passes me and Wes and then Sammy, and Victoria and Teresa. They're not going that fast, but they're faster than me. I try not to think about the fact that they've probably stepped in some of the poop piles without even minding.

Coach T is clapping for everyone, and when Sanjit passes I tag along with him like nothing happened at all.

We reach the starting point and join the others and that's when Victoria sings out, "Joseph only did one lap."

Everybody looks at me, and I wait.

"Joseph did what Joseph could do today," says Coach T. She has that tone that she has sometimes in the Resource Room when she's telling someone to mind their own business, without actually saying that.

When the girls have finished sipping from their Poland Spring bottles and the boys have finished their competition of making the loudest slurp at the water fountain, Coach T says, "Okay, guys. Way to take it slow! Good job. Now we're going on the woods trail. Remember, easy does it. Follow the arrows to White Oak, and I'll meet you at the top of the hill. Walking is fine. I just want you to get familiar with the course. Now, everybody ready?"

There's that silence again.

"Great!" says Coach T. "To the woods!"

Heather is first out again, and I'm still last. I enter the woods, but I don't see any arrows on the trail. They must be covered up by the fallen leaves and pine needles. Victoria and Teresa aren't too far ahead of me, so I figure I'll be okay as long as I keep my eye on them. They're running together slowly, side by side. They both have their hair tied back in ponytails—Teresa's is blond and Victoria's is dark brown—and they're perfectly in sync, bouncing and swinging left, right, left, right with every step. They're like little doggie tails. Left, right, left, right, perfectly together, perfectly in time. Left, right, left, right.

And suddenly I'm on the ground.

I look back at the trail and see a big root sticking up. I guess I tripped. I try to get up, but I'm pinned by my T-shirt to a thornbush. I look ahead and see Victoria's ponytail waving like a last little flag of hope, and then she's out of sight, too.

I brush the dirt off my knees and try to pry my shirtsleeve out of the thornbush's jaws, but it's got me. I'm stuck here, for who knows how long. The bushes are dotted with little red berries. It makes me wonder, *If this were the wilderness and I was lost, could I eat these berries to stay alive?* I read once that there are certain berries that make you throw up. I wonder if these are those kinds. There are some fallen branches in the woods. Could I build a hut with those? If the berries were no good, could I kill an animal and eat it? A fish, maybe. If there was a stream and a fish, I could catch it and probably get myself to eat it if I was on the verge of starvation. But a squirrel or a rabbit? No, I couldn't. Besides, I'd rather share the nuts and berries with them, because it's better to have a little animal companion than to be all alone. Maybe I could even train a squirrel to gather nuts and seeds and share them with me. That would be fun.

I don't know how much time has passed when I hear a voice.

"Joseph." I look up. It's Heather. She doesn't look happy to see me. I hear kids' voices coming toward us.

"He got lost in the woods?" one is saying.

"How could he get lost? It's only one path."

"What happened?" Heather asks.

"Um, I fell," I answer, "and then I guess I got distracted."

"Distracted?"

"It's a problem I have."

"Yeah, well, we've all got problems." She tugs my shirt away from the thornbush, then puts out her hand and pulls me up.

Wes and Sammy are coming down the path. "Hey, man," says Sammy. "We thought maybe you were eaten by snakes."

"Or a Komodo dragon."

"Let's go," says Heather, like she doesn't have time for all this silliness, and she takes off. I stumble behind her and so do Wes and Sammy. We're out of the woods in about two minutes. I got lost on a trail that takes two minutes to run.

But now there's the hill. White Oak Lane. Sammy, Wes, and I stand there at the bottom and watch with amazement as Heather bounds up.

"Did Coach T tell you guys to come find me?" I ask.

"No," says Sammy. "Coach is up top. It was her."

"Who?" I ask.

"That new girl. Heather. She said we should wait, and then you didn't come out."

Wes is looking up the hill. "We've got to run up this thing?" he asks.

"I guess," says Sammy.

"Oh, Mama," says Wes.

Sammy narrows his eyes and decides to take the hill in a sprint. Wes puts his head down and follows him. I start heading up, but it feels like the time in gym when Charlie Kastner snuck up behind me and put his hand on my shoulder just when I was trying to get up from sitting cross-legged. Gravity is even worse than Charlie Kastner. And then that pain in my side comes back.

All I can do is walk up, with a little spurt of a jog every few steps. By the time I get to the top I'm clutching my side and gasping for air. I have little, itchy scratches from the thorn-bush and I feel like I've rolled through a mud puddle.

Coach T is leading the rest of the team in a few push-ups and sit-ups on the grass.

"Good job, Joseph! I knew you could do it!" she says in her super-encouraging Mrs. T voice. I get down to try a push-up, but an acorn digs into my hand and my arm muscles just give a little spasm and collapse.

I just stay there on the ground. I think I might throw up.

A few minutes later, Coach T claps her hands and tells us we all did a great job. Practice is finished. I roll over and look up. Heather appears over me.

"Why did you bother to find me?" I ask. "Why didn't you leave me to starve in the woods? It would feel better than this."

"Coach told me to," she says.

"Coach was up here."

Heather shrugs. "So I took pity on you." She looks me over and says, "Have an orange."

So now it's an orange. I still don't know what she means, but it doesn't matter. It doesn't matter that I got past the goose poop, or that I didn't die in the woods, or that I made it up the hill. I've had enough of being slow and tired and in pain. I've had enough of being rescued and told to eat fruit.

I peel myself off the ground and start the walk home.

I decide that that's it. This can't go on. I have to think up a reason for quitting cross country, before it kills me.

CHAPTER 12

THE PERFECT EXCUSE TO AVOID PRACTICE presents itself the next morning.

"So, Superhero," says Grandpa, "I have to get a few things from Sunset. Want to help me this afternoon after school?"

"Sure!" I say, much too happily.

"You won't have too much homework?"

I always have too much homework, but I say, "No more than usual," which isn't quite a lie. I'm glad he doesn't ask me about practice. That one's a yes-or-no question.

"I have to get my reading glasses and my laptop," says Grandpa. "I'll appreciate the company."

"You have a laptop?" I ask.

"You think I was born yesterday?" he answers. "So, I'll see you after school and we'll ruffle some geriatric feathers." Whatever that means, I'm glad I can skip practice to do it.

When school is over, I leave in a hurry so Mrs. T won't see me and make me feel guilty. I'll explain tomorrow.

At home, Grandpa is waiting outside. Dad walks to work when the weather is nice, so we can use his old Volvo to drive

to Sunshine Senior Living. It's a short drive, and when we walk in there's a skinny lady standing inside at a desk marked "Reception." She's gripping her hands together in front of her chest. When she sees Grandpa, her face gets pruney.

"Mr. Schatzkis. You're back," she says.

"Just picking up a few things," says Grandpa. "I'm not staying, so don't get excited."

I think that's a joke, but if it is, she doesn't seem to appreciate his humor.

We pass the dining room and even though it's only about 3:30, there are lots of people there already, like dinner is just around the corner. They're sitting at tables with white tablecloths and the carpet is red, green, and black with all sorts of swirly patterns and wiggly shapes. There are chandeliers hanging from the ceiling.

"This is fancy, Grandpa. It looks like a movie or something."

"The *Titanic*, maybe," he says.

I look around. There are more women than men, and lots of walkers are parked around the room, some with little gray rubber feet, some with wheels. The ones with wheels have hand brakes, like bicycles. They look like giant insects or alien creatures, except with big old-lady bags hanging off the handles.

Grandpa squints as he looks in. He motions with his head

toward a group of old people at a table in the corner. There are three men and about seven women. Two of the men are just in plain white undershirts. One has skinny arms, but the other one's arms are big and chubby, with hair even up on his shoulders.

"There they are," he says. "The same as when I left."

"Who?" I ask.

"The old guys at that table. The ROMEOs," says Grandpa.

"They don't look like Romeos."

"That's what they call themselves. The ROMEOs. Retired Old Men Eating Out. Once a week, they go out to a restaurant. Big whoop. They're in Independent Living, so they think they're hot stuff. You go into Assisted, they drop you like a hot tamale."

"Who drops you?"

"The ladies. They don't want to sign on to a lost cause."

"Does Assisted mean you're a lost cause?"

"Well, on a downward spiral, anyway. What they call Independent Living, you can cook, go shopping, take your pills. Assisted Living, they bring you down to meals, stand behind you when you take your pills, and tell you when your shirt is dirty. What comes next . . ." His hand makes a quick backward sweep through the air, like he doesn't even want to think about what comes next.

"What comes next, Grandpa?" I ask with a gulp.

"They call it Nursing Care. I call it 'Just Bury Me Now.'"

I'm starting to see why he doesn't want to go back to Sunshine. "So . . ." I ask, "your room is in the first one, right? Independent."

"Do I look like I'm in Assisted?"

"No," I say.

"You're damn right."

"Are you a ROMEO?"

"Am I rushing over there to say hello?"

"No."

"Then you can assume I'm not a ROMEO."

"Oh," I say. "Why not?"

"Why not," he responds, thinking. "Well, first of all, there's Monty." He's looking at the man in the red shirt. He has hair that looks like a strip of dryer lint. "Retired lawyer. For not the nicest guys. Does he think he's fooling somebody with that hair? One good breeze, it's gone with the wind."

"Who are the others?"

"That's Ronny. The skinny one. Fighting Assisted like a fish caught on a line. Can't remember what day it is, but the girls think he's handsome, so they cover for him. And Sig." He waves his finger in the direction of the one with the hairy shoulders. "Manufactured ladies' pants for forty years. Thinks we all want to hear about it. Bell-bottoms, straight leg, capri pants. He could talk your ear off with those capri pants. We used to call them pedal pushers. What's the big deal?"

Then Grandpa spots another man. He's sitting at a table by himself. When I look at him, and then back at the ROMEOs, I can't help thinking that Sunshine Senior Living isn't that different from middle school. There's the cool table. The popular kids. Then there's the guy sitting alone.

Grandpa motions for me to follow him and we go over there.

"Eddie," he says.

Eddie looks up. "Fred, they found you," he says, smiling. "I hear they called the FBI."

"I turned myself in. I didn't like life on the run," says Grandpa. He shakes Eddie's hand and then pushes me forward. "This is my grandson, Joseph." Eddie reaches out a bony hand and I shake it. I think it's going to feel cold and dry, but it's actually strong and warm. "Joseph is sheltering me for the time being, but what do you say we find ourselves a nice bachelor pad and live it up in our declining years?"

Eddie's smile fades a little and he shakes his head.

"Eddie," Grandpa says, sitting next to him, "I know you're missing Emily. When Sophie died, my heart broke in a million pieces. I didn't eat, I didn't sleep. But we have to live."

"I'm living, I'm living," says Eddie. "I like the food. And there's a tai chi class that really gets the blood pumping." He stretches one arm out and dangles the other over his head.

Grandpa is about to answer, but then I see his eyebrows go up as a chubby little woman with a walker charges toward us. If I'm right, and the ROMEOs are the cool kids and Eddie is the loner, then here comes the Mean Girl.

"I'll see you later, Eddie," says Grandpa. He stands up to go, but it's too late.

"It's him!" says the lady, pointing a shaky finger. She's moving pretty fast for a lady with a walker. "It's him! Schatzkis from Atlantic City. Two hours we waited, but Mr. Big Shot didn't show."

"Joey," Grandpa says, "follow me." We head out the nearest door, scoot around the corner, and hurry down a hallway. We can hear the woman's voice, but her walker doesn't even have wheels, so I'm pretty sure we can outrun her. On our left is the men's room, and we duck in.

There's a man standing at the urinal, but he doesn't turn around. I think we've gotten away. But a second later the door opens and it's her.

"Oh, you think you can hide!" she yells. "Think again, Mr. Big Shot! Thinks he's too good for the Sunshine group. Has to go off on his own in Atlantic City and leave the chaperone thinking he's dead!"

The skinny lady from the front has followed her in. "Mrs. Fligle. Please," she says. "This is the men's room."

"Let this *alter cocker* drop his pants and see if I bat an eyelash. He kept us all waiting two hours in Atlantic City."

"I know, Mrs. Fligle. We all know." She gives Grandpa a look. "But there's another gentleman in here . . ."

"Deaf as a post," says Mrs. Fligle. "He doesn't even know we're here." I guess she's right, because the man still hasn't turned to look. Now he's moved over to wash his hands.

"It's still the men's room," says the skinny lady. "And Mr. Schatzkis is just here to pick up some things. He's not staying. Right, Mr. Schatzkis?"

"Wouldn't dream of it," says Grandpa.

"If I were you, I'd stay out of here for good!" snaps Mrs. Fligle. "Don't stay where you're not wanted!"

Grandpa looks a little like I do when I'm trying not to mind. But I can see him flinch as Mrs. Fligle hurls those words at him. The fact is, even if you don't want to go to their stupid party, it makes you feel bad to know you're not invited. At least in middle school, they whisper behind your back. Here, they just blurt it right out to your face.

The skinny lady finally eases Mrs. Fligle out the door, and I breathe a sigh of relief.

"I guess mean girls get even meaner when they grow up," I say to Grandpa.

The man who's been washing his hands finally turns around. "Your grandson?" he asks.

Grandpa nods and says, "Joseph."

"Eh?" says the man.

"Joseph!" Grandpa yells.

"He's a smart boy," he says, and shuffles his way out of the bathroom. It's not something I hear very often. I smile and wave.

Grandpa peeks out the bathroom door and motions for me to follow him. We scurry into the elevator, and when we come out on the second floor we go straight to his room. I stand guard outside while he's getting his laptop, just in case Mrs. Fligle tries to hunt him down again.

When Grandpa comes out, he stops for a second and looks down the hallway. It's decorated with soft-colored paintings, all light blues and pinks and peaches. They're the kind of colors that tell you everything's fine. Or, as my mother says, "Just fine." The floors are the color of watery lemonade and there's a handrail along the wall.

It doesn't seem like a place for Grandpa. The house he lived in with Grandma had a bright red checkered sofa and a flowery rug and walls covered in pine. I wonder if he's remembering that, too. Whatever he's thinking, it takes him a minute before he turns and shuts the door to his room with a thunk.

Then he turns to me. "Come on," he says. "Let's split this joint."

As we wave to the skinny lady at the front desk, I realize: I've gotten to help Grandpa with his jailbreak after all.

CHAPTER 13

THE FIRST THING I DO WHEN I GET TO THE
Resource Room the next morning is tell Mrs. T why I had
to miss practice yesterday. She says something about family
coming first, but I think she knows it's an excuse. I don't have
the heart to tell her that I might not come today, either. Or
tomorrow. Or the next day.

When I get to French, Heather doesn't look at me. She's
busy drawing something. Just as Madame Labelle starts class
with a big "*Bonjour*," Heather holds up the notebook so I can
see.

It's me, as a chicken.

"I am not a chicken!" I blurt out.

"*Monsieur! Mademoiselle!*" Madame Labelle calls out, using
two of the few French words I know. The class is giggling.

Then Heather looks right at Madame Labelle and starts
talking. In French. I catch the words for *please*, which sound
like "silver plate," but the rest is a mystery to me, except for,
"Friedman," and something that sounds like "important."

There's silence. Madame looks dumbfounded by all that

French pouring out of Heather's mouth. Then she motions with her hand like she's shooing a dog away and says something that sounds like "allay." Heather grabs me by the arm and pulls me out the door.

Out in the hallway, I squirm away from her. "What was all that?"

"All what?"

"All those French sounds."

"I said we needed to talk." She's acting like it's normal to have weird gargly stuff tumble out of your mouth like you're from another planet.

"So why are you in here if you know French?"

"We did French in fifth grade, but they said it didn't count."

"That's stupid," I say. "If—"

"Hey!" she interrupts. "I'm not the problem here."

I guess that means I am.

"Where were you yesterday? Why weren't you at practice?"

"I . . . I couldn't . . . come," I stutter.

"One tough practice and you chicken out." She's looking at me with squinty eyes, like she can't believe how useless I am.

"I was with my grandpa," I say, trying to convince us both that I had a good excuse. "He needed help getting stuff from his senior living place." Then I throw in what I hope will impress her or distract her or both. "He just got out of jail."

She isn't impressed or distracted.

"Did you tell him you had practice?"

I pause long enough for her to know that the answer is no.

"You know you need ten practices to qualify for the first meet. Coach told us, or didn't you hear?"

"Ten practices?" I say. Of course I didn't hear. Add it to the list.

"You can't just skip one because you're tired, or scared, or . . ."

"I wasn't scared."

Heather looks at me like she knows the truth. But ten practices? Maybe that's the answer. If I can't make ten practices, I can't be on the team. I just have to think up why I can't. Then I have it.

"Oh, no," I say. "Hebrew school! I can't possibly make ten practices. I have Hebrew school starting next week. I'll have to miss Wednesdays, so . . ."

"We get Wednesdays off," Heather says. "You can still make ten practices, without Wednesdays."

I try to think of some other excuse. Homework? Grandpa? Goose poop allergy? But what comes out is the truth. "What if I don't want to? What if I don't want to run in the first race? What if I don't want to be on the team?"

"Fine," she says with a slow blink. "Quitter."

"I'm not a quitter," I say, even though that's exactly what I seem to be.

"It sounds to me like you are. A chicken quitter." She's turning to go back into the classroom.

"But I stink," I say, probably too loud. "I stink at running, like I stink at everything else."

Heather turns around. "You've only been to one practice. You haven't even tried," she says.

"I have, too."

"Then try harder."

"I can't try any harder!" I yell at her. "You know how many times I've heard that? Every year, every teacher. 'You've got to try harder, Joseph.' 'You're not working hard enough, Joseph.' I work and I try all the time, and I never get better at anything. All that happens is that I stay terrible and everybody makes fun of me."

"Nobody was making fun of you," says Heather.

"Oh yeah? Go have a banana, Joseph. Go eat an orange!" I know I must sound like a maniac. I'm surprised doors aren't flying open up and down the hallway.

"That wasn't making fun," she says.

"Yeah? What was it, then?"

She sighs. "You had a stitch, right?"

"A what?"

"A stitch. That pain in your side."

I remember now, that's what Mrs. T called it. "Yeah."

"Your potassium level was low. Your body was working really hard and that's what happens. You get a stitch. I've had them, too. Lots of times. Bananas have potassium. That's why I told you to eat a banana."

"Oh," I say. I feel really stupid.

"Oranges, too," she adds. I feel even stupider.

"But go ahead and quit if it's too hard." Then she mumbles, "Let everybody down."

"Who am I letting down?" Then I add, "Besides myself," thinking she's giving me that old line.

"The whole team," she says. "I guess that's another thing you didn't hear Coach say. The athletic department won't run the program unless we have ten kids. Not that I care if it's you," she adds, "it's just that you happen to be number ten. But if you want to give up, go ahead. We'll find someone else."

Then she stares hard at me and says, "I wasn't expecting much from you, Friedman, but I was expecting more than that."

I feel my mouth open, but nothing comes out. Not only was she not teasing me, she was expecting something. Even if it wasn't much, she was actually expecting something from me.

"*Mademoiselle, Monsieur.*" Madame Labelle is sticking her head out into the hallway. "Silver plate."

"*Oui, Madame,*" says Heather. Then she says something

else in French to Madame Labelle and turns back to me. "That means, 'We're finished,'" she says.

Madame Labelle goes back inside, but she leaves the door open. I'm weighing my options: Running vs. not running. Pain, failure, and humiliation vs. rejection. Right now, rejection feels the worst.

"I can still make the ten practices? Before the first meet?" I ask.

"Yeah," she says.

"Okay," I blurt out. "I'll try."

"All right." She whacks me on the arm and I try to smile. "By the way, what was your grandpa in jail for?"

I consider telling her that he's an outlaw-bank-robber-wanted-by-the-FBI jewel thief. Instead, I say, "He left his senior living group in Atlantic City. He went to Caesar's."

She nods. "Nice."

I follow her back into French class and sit down. Like it or not, I'm back on the team, with nine more practices to go. And that's just to get to the starting line.

CHAPTER 14

I START A RUNNING DIARY. IT LOOKS LIKE THIS:

Practice 1—Goose poop. Pain in side. Lost in the woods.

Practice 2—Sunshine Senior Living (missed practice).

Practice 3—Back to practice. Ran the course again. Goose poop has been cleared, but stitch came back. Collapsed on hill.

Practice 4—Rain. Mud eats my shoe.

Practice 5—Coach's advice—go straight instead of weaving around like a drunk. Harder than it seems.

Practice 6—Up White Oak hill twice. Did not die, but close.

Practice 7—More rain. Worms on track. Coach T lets me run on grass instead of on the worms, so I don't throw up.

That's all the diary writing I can do. Mrs. T—she's still Mrs. T in the Resource Room—always tells us that when we do something that doesn't come out so well, we should think about what we learned from the experience. What I've learned from keeping a running diary is that I'm not good at diary writing. Those diary books with the stick drawings

look easy to do, but they're not. When I try to draw stick figures, they look like stick figures. I can't make them look like they have feelings.

If I could, I'd show my stick figure looking exhausted, frustrated, and slow.

But diary or no diary, I somehow finish my tenth practice and qualify for our first meet. Not that I'm convinced this is totally a good thing.

When that last practice finally ends, Coach T turns to Sammy. "Oh, I almost forgot, Sammy," she says. "What was it that you kept asking me about? Was it uniforms?"

Sammy's eyes open wide. "Yes!" he shouts.

"Then follow me," says Coach T.

She leads us toward the teachers' parking lot, which is up the concrete stairs and across the practice field. Even though the stair monster tries to tip me backward into its waiting jaws, I hang on to the railing and pull myself up, cracked step by cracked step. My shoelace comes undone around step number nine, but I push on to the top. I stop to tie it, and when I look up, the rest of the team is already across the field.

Ahead, to my left, the football team is running a drill. They're in two lines facing each other, and one by one they run to the middle of the field and smash in the center. Then they stagger back in line to wait their turns to do it again. Even though I know that the kids inside the shoulder pads and helmets are guys like Charlie Kastner, and I really don't care what happens to his head or his shoulders or anything else, I can't help flinching each time they crash.

I walk by, grateful that they're too busy smashing into each other to notice me.

Coach Papasian looks very content. The louder the crunch, the happier he is. He claps his hands together and nods and calls out, "Attaway!"

To my right, I catch sight of a bee, buzzing around the clover flowers in the grass. It's one of those really fat, fuzzy, yellow-and-black bumblebees. I read somewhere that they don't sting unless you annoy them, but since I don't know what this particular bumblebee would find to be annoying, I won't get too close. The bee is so peaceful, especially compared to the smashing and crunching going on at the football practice. I crouch down to see it better. It's beautiful, the way it sits on one little toasted marshmallow of a flower, sucks out some nectar, and floats on to the next.

The bee is happily drinking when clomp, a foot lands on it. A big, terrible foot in a dirty, cleated football shoe. I jump to my feet.

"Friedman," says Charlie Kastner. I guess getting thwacked in the middle of the field isn't enough to keep him from wobbling over here, after all. "Hey Friedman! You watching grass grow or something?"

I'm staring at his shoe. The bee is under there. A minute ago it was all carefree, flower hopping, and now it's another of Charlie's victims.

"Friedman, I'm talking to you."

I don't even look up at his helmet-framed face. I try to channel my energy into some interspecies SOS, signaling the bee's friends to come in an angry swarm and chase Charlie away. A thousand bees. A thousand stings.

I picture that poor bee, suffocating or, worse yet, squashed. Before I even think what I'm doing, I nudge Charlie's shoe with my toe. He doesn't move, and I nudge it again. Finally, the shoe lifts up and like a miracle, the bee flies away. It must've been stuck in the grass, hiding between cleats, not smashed at all, just trapped.

Free! It's free. But my urge to rejoice is zapped when I realize that Charlie is staring at me in disbelief.

"Did you just kick me?" he says. I look for the bee. Maybe it knows I'm its hero and is staging a sneak attack. But no, it's gone. "Answer me, Friedman. Did you just kick me? You did, didn't you? You kicked my foot. Are you actually picking a fight with me?"

The answer is so obviously, so emphatically no that I can't even get it out of my mouth.

"Well, I'm impressed, Friedman. Really. I'm so impressed, I'll give you the first punch. For free."

"Get back in line, Kastner!" calls Coach Papasian, but there's no way Charlie is going anywhere.

"Frappaolo over there just gave me a good hit, got it started for you. Now's your chance. Punch me. Go on, punch me. Right here in the stomach. You get a free shot."

I don't know what to do. A bunch of the guys on the football team are watching now. If I run away, they'll tell the whole school. I look at Charlie's stomach, and I know I'll regret it, but I throw out my fist as hard as I can.

My hand socks right into something hard and plastic, which hurts like crazy. Then Charlie pushes forward, so even as I punch him I'm getting thrown backward, and before I know it I'm on the ground and half the football team is doubled over with laughter.

"Kastner!" calls Coach Papasian.

"Hey, sorry, Friedman. I'd like to stay and finish this, but I've got to go." He looks down the field, gives a sort of chin salute, and smiles. "Say hi to Miss Hip Check," he says, and waddles away, back to his football buddies.

I'm still on the ground when I see Heather. She's coming back to get me. Again.

"Well, I showed him," I say, rubbing my hand. It really hurts.

"Yeah, that backward-fall trick works every time," says Heather. I guess she saw the whole thing. I pull myself up, and she swats some scrunched leaves off my back.

"I wish I was stronger," I say as we walk toward the parking lot. "Or at least fast. If you can't fight, at least you should be able to run away. "

"It wouldn't matter," says Heather. "They find a way."

The parking lot isn't far, and when Coach T and the other kids see us, they wave and call to us to hurry up. There's no need to tell them what just happened. The story will be all over school in about three and a half seconds.

Sammy is actually jumping up and down. Coach T stands behind her car, which has tiny headlights that make it look surprised to see us. It's a faded silvery blue, and when I get there I can't help running my finger along the side door, just to see if silver dust comes off on my finger. It doesn't.

Coach T sings out a little trumpet call, "Ta ta ta ta ta, ta-tah!" Then she opens the trunk with a flourish and takes out a canvas bag. She fishes out the light blue uniforms one by one, holding them up to see the size and calling our names.

"You each get a singlet," she says, handing them out, "and shorts. They're brand-new. Take care of them."

I have never heard the word "singlet" before, but now I'm holding one. It's made out of some satiny material that's so slippery it pours through my hands and onto the ground. That happens twice, and then I roll it up with the shorts and put them both into my backpack. Together, they hardly make up a handful.

Then Coach T takes out a big black garbage bag. She pulls out an armload of sweatpants and sets them down, then holds a sweatshirt up, so we can see the front. It says "Lakeview XC" and there's a leopard in white.

"What's 'XC'?" asks Victoria.

"Cross country," explains Coach T. "'X' like 'cross,' and 'C' for 'country.'" She looks at the labels and after about five, she says, "Looks like they're all XL."

"I thought you said XC," says Mark.

"No, XL in size. Extra large." She puts her hand up on her head for a few seconds and then shrugs. "Oh, well," she says in a not-unhappy way. "They'll be way too big, but we're going to have some cold afternoons. I'll try to reorder for winter, but for now it's better than nothing."

She hands them out quickly, since they're all the same. They're huge and soft and the blue color of a Rice Krispies box. I take mine and run my fingers over the sandpapery plastic paint that spells out "Lakeview XC" in white. The leopard is white, too, and they've left holes in the paint, so the spots are the color of the sweatshirt. Really, it could be a puma with fleas, but I know it's a leopard. Its back is curved and its legs are stretched out, like it's chasing a deer or a wildebeest.

Mark and Sanjit are stuffing their uniforms into their backpacks and looking around for their rides home. It's already pickup time, and cars are pulling into the lot. Victoria holds the singlet up to her shoulders and does a slinky fashion-show walk so her mom can see her new outfit. Erica's mother is laughing at the enormous sweatshirt, which will probably reach Erica's shins.

Heather is standing by herself, on the weedy cement island that divides the parking lot. She's watching those girls and their mothers. When she sees me watching her, she waves, and I hold up my uniform in triumph. She gives a quick thumbs-up, rolls up her uniform, sticks it under her arm, and heads off in a run.

I stuff my sweatshirt into my backpack and start the walk home. I wonder how ridiculous I'll look. The sweatshirt will come down to my knees. At least. The leopard doesn't even have real spots, and nobody is going to understand what "XC" means.

I think back to what Coach T said. For now, it's better than nothing. I stop and pull out my uniform, just to make sure I didn't leave anything behind: sweatshirt, sweatpants, shorts, singlet. They're all here.

I have ten practices under my belt and I'm still standing. I have a team uniform right here in my hands. Spots or no spots, I am a Lakeview Leopard.

It is so much better than nothing.

CHAPTER 15

WHEN I GET BACK HOME, GRANDPA IS CON-veniently occupied in the bathroom. His staying with us has worked out pretty well. My mom has been super busy. At A La Maison: Home and Kitchen, every holiday starts early, so even though it's still September, they're practically finished with Halloween and already putting up the Thanksgiving displays. Christmas will start in October, and Valentine's Day will get going in late December. So she's been working pretty hard lately. Dad has a new dental suction unit that's selling like hotcakes, so he's been working extra hard, too. It makes my parents feel better to know that Grandpa will be here when I get home.

But today, I need some time alone. I tiptoe past the bathroom, into my room, and ease the door shut. I drop the sweats on my bed and pull the singlet and shorts out of my backpack. I can't wait to try them on.

The shorts are tiny, barely even as big as underwear. They look like they could fit my teddy bear, Wilson. I take off my shirt and jeans and try the shorts first. I guess my waist

isn't that much bigger than Wilson's, and the elastic is super stretchy, so they feel fine. I take a practice run around my room, lifting my knees as high as they'll go, doing a few circles around the end of the bed. So far, so good.

The singlet seems to be a piece of clothing that hardly exists. When I slip it over my head, I feel like there's more armhole and neck opening than shirt. But at the same time, it hangs down practically to my knees. I try tucking it into the little tiny shorts and somehow it all miraculously fits.

My excitement immediately dims when I turn and stare at myself in the mirror: My skinny arms and legs. My bony chest and shoulders. If I had any summer tan, it's all faded and I'm about the color of a raw cashew. I flex to see if I can round out my limbs with manly muscles. All that does is make my arms look like the middle section of a chicken wing.

I wouldn't blame Charlie Kastner for laughing at me. I would laugh at me. My feet look like flippers. My dad keeps telling me that means I'm due for my growth spurt, and that he spurted right around the age I am now. I keep watching and waiting, but so far no spurt. Not even close.

I've had *Get in Shape, Boys!* stashed under my bed for more than two weeks now. I haven't had the nerve to pick it up and look inside. I'm afraid I'll find a special chapter for kids like me entitled "Lost Cause: Is This You?" I think about those guys on the cover. I can't imagine how this matchstick of a body could possibly turn into one like that. But the uniform and the practices aren't doing the trick, so I guess it's time for more serious measures.

I almost pull a muscle just picking it up. It's four-hundred-something pages with thirty-something chapters and each chapter has about a million sections. Not only are the guys in this book fit and handsome, but if they read this book to get that way, they must be speed readers, too.

The chapters start out friendly enough, but get scarier as you go on:

"Looking Your Best."

"Taking Care of Your Pearly Whites."

"The Strange Land of Puberty."

"Overcoming Acne."

"Hair Removal."

Hair Removal?

There are chapters on smoking cigarettes, taking drugs, and using steroids. I don't really need any more warnings on those. I'm already terrified of all those things. There's a chapter on being a vegan, which is kind of scary in its own way.

There are sections on birth control and sexually transmitted diseases, which I skip over so frantically I almost rip the pages.

When I finally get to Part II, I find it:

"Getting in Shape."

I look pretty carefully, but I don't see anything about running. What I do find is:

"Calisthenics and Pumping Iron: Your Path to Strength and Confidence!"

In this section our guide is a guy named Pete Power. He's some kind of official "Pumping Iron" instructor, and he's a lot older than the kids on the cover. He's not even a teenager. In the pictures, he demonstrates sit-ups and push-ups and lifting weights. He pushes and twists and pulls, smiling through it all like he's in a shaving commercial. Even when he's just stretching, his muscles are round and smooth and shiny, and piled on top of each other like a three-scoop ice cream cone. And he must have read the chapter on hair removal, because even though he's a grown man, there's not a tuft to be seen.

He demonstrates lifting dumbbells and barbells with weights the size of manhole covers stacked about five deep. Then he puts on belts and straps and gloves to use some giant padded exercise machines. In one picture he shows off his stomach, which is rippled with abdominal muscles, or "abs" for short.

To top it all off, he gives pieces of advice: "Be courteous to other athletes," he says, "wash your clothes after each workout." Sounds like a good rule.

I put the book on the floor and look in the mirror. I untuck my singlet and check for abs.

Hopeless.

There's a knock on the door. "Joseph?" It's Grandpa.

"Oh, hey, Grandpa," I say as casually as I can, but it comes out in a particularly squeaky, guilty voice.

"You okay in there?" he asks. "Guess you snuck by me."

"Sure!" I say. "I'm fine!" I throw my sweats on to cover my skinny self and waddle to the door. Then I remember *Get in Shape, Boys!*, so I dash over and shove it underneath the bed with my foot. Or at least I try to. It's stuck on something, probably an old boot or a "Pirates of the Caribbean" plastic sword from our trip last winter.

"Joseph?"

"Coming!" I call and give *Get in Shape, Boys!* another few jabs with my toe, leaving it about half hidden and my big toe throbbing. I waddle over to the door and scrunch the extra-long sweatshirt arms up around my elbows so I can have a hand free to let Grandpa in.

Grandpa wanders over to my bed and sits down, his left foot practically nudging *Get in Shape, Boys!* He folds his hands and looks me over. I must look like a lumpy pillow, or a powder-blue Michelin Man. He has a little half smile on his face, but at least he doesn't laugh at me.

"So," I say, sitting down on the other side of the bed. I try to casually cross my legs, but the sweatpants are way too bulky. "Did you have a good day? Keeping busy?" My mother asked

Grandpa that a few days ago, but as it comes out of my mouth I think it sounds really dumb.

"Well," says Grandpa, "I took a walk, went to get some new white socks—the kind without the tight elastic . . ." I nod. I hate those, too. "Then I took another walk and read the paper. Not what you'd call thrilling. How about you?"

"We got our uniforms," I say.

"So I see," he says.

"These are just the sweats. They all came in extra large."

I'm starting to see why these things are called sweats. I feel a drip under my arm and on my forehead. If I don't take them off soon, I might pass out. So, I really have no choice but to pull the sweatshirt over my head, step out of the sweatpants, and bare my skinny self to Grandpa. "We have our first meet tomorrow," I say, shifting a little, trying to look like Pete Power but probably looking closer to one of those stick figures I can't draw.

"Your first meet," he says. "That's exciting. Are you nervous?"

"Well, yeah," I say. "But I get nervous about pretty much everything. Last year the school psychologist told me I have something called anticipatory anxiety."

"You have who?" asks Grandpa.

"Anticipatory anxiety. It means I worry about things that might happen. She wrote it down for me," I say, fishing a bright yellow piece of notepaper out of my night-table drawer.

I hold it up to show Grandpa. "She said it would help if I knew what my problem was."

"Did it?"

"Not really. I just worried a lot about having it."

Ms. Porter's note is stapled to a piece of lined paper covered in my own writing. She told me to make myself a "worry list" so we could talk about it. I didn't realize she meant a list of things I was worried about. I thought she meant a list that would help me worry. So I wrote this:

- It's never too early to start worrying.
- Nothing is too little or unimportant.
- If you have an uneasy feeling, try to pinpoint what's bothering you. That way you can focus on it and worry properly.
- Worry expands to fill available time.
- Even if something's already happened, you can still worry about it.

I thought it was a pretty impressive list, but Ms. Porter didn't seem to like it very much. Grandpa is watching me as I look it over. Somehow he seems to know that my worries right now have to do with my puny biceps and bony limbs.

"You know," says Grandpa, like he's telling me a secret,

"looking at you in that uniform? It reminds me of some men I've seen on TV."

"Seriously?" I say, horrified. "You mean this could be permanent?" I can't believe I could look like a walking skeleton my whole life.

"Wait a second, Superhero. I was going to say, there are professional athletes who look like you."

"Really? Who?"

"Marathon runners. The ones who win—in New York, Boston, the Olympics even. They're skin, bone, muscle—nothing extra to weigh them down."

I look in the mirror again, this time holding my arms in a running position. There's certainly not much to weigh me down.

"You do some sit-ups, some push-ups, keep up your running, you'll be Mr. Marathon before you know it." He gets up and says, "And meanwhile, I thought I'd toast up some of those frozen waffles. When you're finished in here, maybe you'll come join me."

I suddenly realize I'm starving. Waffles seem like the answer to every question. Waffles with maple syrup. Waffles with peanut butter and jelly. In fact, you could put spinach on top of one and I'd probably eat it.

I give Grandpa a thumbs-up and he gives one back. A few seconds later, I hear the shunk of the toaster handle going down.

Skin, bone, and muscle. I get down on the rug and do some

push-ups. I stand up and examine my arms in the mirror.

Still skinny.

I lock my feet under the bed and do some sit-ups. The bed frame is digging into the tops of my feet and my stomach muscles are cramping up, so I stop after six. I pull up my shirt and look in the mirror.

No change.

I put my regular clothes back on, and give *Get in Shape, Boys!* one more shove, this time making sure it goes all the way under my bed. I toss my singlet and shorts under there, too, but then I pull them back out and stuff them into my backpack. The meet is tomorrow, and it would be just like me to forget.

I think about what Grandpa said. Marathons. Why didn't I think of that? Maybe marathons are my destiny. Maybe being a walking Q-Tip will pay off in the end. Once I get better at cross country, I can build up to longer distances and then I'll run a marathon. How far is a marathon? Five miles? Ten? I lie down on my bed and imagine it. Me, finishing a marathon, while Pete Power lumbers along, his rounded, muscly body weighing him down.

The smell of Eggos and syrup wafts into my room. As I race to the kitchen, I think about what Mrs. T always says: To achieve every goal, there has to be a first step.

I'll make being a marathoner my new goal. And tomorrow's meet is my first step.

CHAPTER 16

I START THE DAY WITH BANANAS IN MY CEREAL
and a glass of orange juice, and since there are strawberries
in the refrigerator, I throw those into the bowl, too. I'm practically a walking fruit salad.

Today is our first meet, and I'm ready to start my journey
toward my marathon goal.

"Hey, Dad?" I ask, because he knows a lot of things. "How
far is a marathon?"

"Twenty-six miles," he answers, picking up his briefcase.

"Twenty-six miles?" I gulp.

"Twenty-six point two, actually. Why?"

I sigh. "Never mind."

Sometimes I think goals are overrated.

"Well, good luck today!" he says. "I know you'll do great.
Whenever you're ready to have us cheer you on, just say the
word."

"Okay," I answer. I've stuffed my mouth full of Cheerios, so
it sounds more like "Mmmkkmmphhh."

When I told my mom and dad I was doing cross country

they were really excited. They wanted to come to all of my meets. I pointed out that they'd have to leave work super early since nearly all the meets were at other schools, and also, since we run through the woods, there's really not much to see. They still wanted to come, but then I told them I'd get really nervous, and I might trip and fall and break something. That seemed to do the trick. At least for now.

My mom's going to Maison late today, so she gives me a kiss and I walk to school by myself. I'm in a daze—not that I'm normally Mr. Focus—but all I can think about is the meet.

When I pass Victoria in the hall, she actually puts up her hand for a high five. In the Resource Room, Erica, Sanjit, and I are a chorus of bouncing legs and tapping pencils. In French, Heather is drawing the team as tortoises and hares. Of course I'm a tortoise, but I don't mind, especially because she has me sweating, gritting my teeth, and crossing the finish line.

Finally, after my last class, I duck into a bathroom stall and change into my uniform. Then I run to join the others in front of the gym. I feel like I'm having one of those dreams where I'm out in public half naked. Except, I really am out in public half naked.

Wes, Mark, and Sanjit are already clustered together, wearing their uniforms. Sanjit's arms are a nice mocha color and Mark's are the color of a French roast coffee bean, but it makes me feel better to see that Wes's arms are even paler and bonier than mine. We fold and unfold our arms and tug at our shorts. We try to look casual, but it's hard to know what to do with our arms and legs. There's so much of them sticking out.

I guess Victoria and Teresa are used to wearing little teensy short shorts, because they seem happy enough. But Brianne isn't the skinniest girl in the world and she has her sweatshirt tied around her waist, even though it's one of those hot, muggy September days that make you think it's still July. Erica is so little that the shorts actually look baggy on her. Heather is sitting on the stairs like she couldn't care less how she looks. If she wanted to know, I'd tell her that she looks fit and strong, but that's probably not what a girl wants to hear. Then again, maybe it is. I figure it's safest not to say anything at all.

Coach T has gone to find out why the bus is late, giving half the school a chance to walk by and snicker at us. We pretend not to hear the comments.

"Nice shorts, Friedman."

"Great look, girls."

"Woo-woo!"

I've never been so happy to see a yellow school bus roll up.

As we race to the door, Sammy comes running. "Sorry I'm late," he says. I stare to figure out what he's wearing. It almost looks like a skirt, but then I realize he's got on red-and-white-checked boxers and they're ballooning out from under his uniform shorts.

"Sammy, what did I tell you?" asks Coach T.

"That some of the world's most successful people are short, so I shouldn't be self-conscious—"

"No, Sammy. What did I tell you about boxer shorts." Sammy looks down. "No jewelry, no watches, no boxer shorts. You're going to have to get some briefs."

"Briefs? You mean tighty-whities? No way! Look, I'll tuck them in." He tries shoving the boxers up into the shorts, but they just puff out again. Victoria and Teresa lean into each other and giggle. Sammy's shoulders droop and he looks down sadly at the red and white checks sticking out.

"Can't your mom bring you some of your brother's?" suggests Mark.

"He's like two sizes smaller than me."

Coach T is looking at her watch and shaking her head. "We've got to go," she says. "I don't want you disqualified, Sammy. Could your mom bring some briefs to New Kingsfield? Could she meet us there?"

Sammy thinks for a minute. Frowning, he says, "Okay, I'll call her."

Coach T claps her hands together. "Excellent! Then let's go!"

I'm nervous. I try to remind myself that I've been to ten practices and run up White Oak Lane about a million times. And I've made progress: now I feel like there are only five angry monkeys hanging on my legs, instead of ten. But I don't know what it will be like at New Kingsfield. Maybe they have hills twice the height of White Oak Lane. Maybe the other kids will laugh at our uniforms. Maybe they'll be twice as fast as we are.

My seat on the bus squeaks with every bump, and my thighs stick to the green plastic. At each turn, I make a wish that we're not there yet. For a while my wishes come true, but unless the driver is a maniac kidnapper or New Kingsfield has been hit by an asteroid, I know eventually my luck will run out.

Mark is sitting next to me, and Heather is across the aisle, staring out the window. Coach T is in front of me.

"Coach?" I say. "Am I going to be the slowest one there?"

She turns around and grips the back of her seat. Her fingernails are almond-shaped and perfectly even. "Don't worry about that," she says. "It's your very first race. Do your best, and whatever you run, it's your personal record." She says this like a personal record is some magical thing. "Once you have that, you can try to do better."

I think about what she's saying. If you're starting from nothing, then anything counts. If I'm terrible, then just ordinary bad will be an improvement. It gives me hope.

Finally, the bus takes one last turn and we arrive. Sammy is looking out the window for his mom. I peel myself from the seat and try to pull down my teeny little shorts as Coach T shoos us off the bus.

The New Kingsfield kids hover around the starting line, along with the team from Hampton. All of them are wearing uniforms just like ours, skimpy little shorts and singlets. New Kingsfield is in red and Hampton is in orange. They're shaking out their arms and legs, and they look nervous and self-conscious and fidgety, too. For a quick moment I'm hit with a strange, unfamiliar feeling, like maybe this is a place where I belong.

We break up into a girls' group and a boys' group, and my group follows a New Kingsfield boy around the course. It's called "walking the course," so we have some idea where we'll be running. There are no woods here; it's just a big, long loop around the field, through the school grounds, and back. As we walk, Sammy keeps an eye on the parking lot.

"My mom's still not here," he says. He pushes the boxers up into his shorts, but they pop back out. We walk around a few buildings and across a field, and when we can see the parking lot again, Sammy's mom still isn't there.

"What do I do?" Sammy asks.

"Go commando," suggests Sanjit.

"What's commando?" asks Sammy.

"Take off the boxers," Mark explains. "Run . . . without them."

"Is that allowed?" I ask.

"Take it off, take it off..." Wes starts to chant, and Sammy smacks him on the arm.

Then Sammy scrunches up his mouth in a determined kind of way, like he's made up his mind. "Where's the bathroom?" he asks.

"Right there," says the New Kingsfield kid, pointing to the building we're passing. "But hurry up, there's not much time."

Wes pulls Sammy along. "We'll meet you guys at the start," he says.

When we get there, the boys are lining up. I stand next to Mark. He's rolling his shoulders, loosening up. A couple of the Hampton kids are staring. They look worried.

"Why are they looking over here?" I ask Mark.

He smiles. "Because they think I'm fast."

"Have they seen you run?"

"Nah. It's because I'm African American," he whispers. "Every sport, it's like, 'Uh-oh, they've got a black kid. He must be good.'" He looks like he sort of enjoys disappointing them.

"Huh. I'm Jewish. Do people expect me to be something?"

"Smart, probably."

"Oh, no," I say, shaking my head. Mark smiles even wider and holds up his hand for a high five. I guess we have something in common.

"All right, gentlemen!" calls out the ref. "Two minutes to the gun."

"Gun?" I say, but nobody answers me.

"Where are Sammy and Wes?" asks Coach T. I'm not used to seeing her look stressed, but she does right now.

"They stopped at the bathroom," says Sanjit.

"The gun is about to go off," says Coach T.

"Gun?" I say again.

Finally, we see them running up from the school building. "Hurry!" calls Coach T.

"One minute!" says the ref.

Wes and Sammy are scampering up the hill. Sammy has his red-and-white boxers in his hand.

The ref takes a gun out of his pocket and holds it in the air. I know it can't be loaded or anything, because this is a track meet, not a fox hunt. But still. He glances at Wes and Sammy and waits a few extra seconds until they make it to the starting line. Sammy tosses the boxers to a surprised Coach T, and we're ready.

I'm sensitive to loud noises, so I cover my ears just to be safe.

"Ready . . ." he says.

A few of the boys bend their knees and get their arms into running position. I keep my hands over my ears.

"Set . . ."

Through my blocked ears, I hear someone calling, "Sammy! Sammy!" I turn to look and take my hands off my ears for a second. A short, chubby woman is running toward us, waving a pair of tighty-whities like a surrender flag.

"I've got them!" she's calling. "Sammy! I've got the underwear!"

BLAM!!!

CHAPTER 17

I CAN'T EVEN BEGIN TO PROCESS WHAT JUST happened. My heart flies out of my eyes, my hands slam back over my ears. I freeze as the others take off. The gunshot is so loud, my nerves are completely jangled, and my pulse is pounding about a zillion beats a second. A zillion and a half.

I hear Coach T's voice, and the girls on the team are shouting, "Run! Go, Joseph, run!" but the best I can do is push myself into a semi-controlled forward fall. I'm down on the ground, then I'm up. My legs are shaking and I go right down again. When I finally feel my feet connecting to the ground I start to run, but I'm so far behind I know I'll never catch up.

The only reason I keep going forward is because I can't turn back. I can hear Heather's voice calling, "Go! Keep going!" My legs are all wobbly and I'm hardly moving, but I don't stop. The other boys are running single file halfway across the field. They're so far away, they look like a trail of ants. Even the slowest ant is about half the field ahead of me.

One by one they start to disappear behind the school building. I keep putting one foot in front of the other until

finally I get there, way behind everybody else. I'm by myself. Everyone is out of sight. I follow the path, hoping this is the way the New Kingsfield kid told us to go, wishing that for once I'd paid attention. I'm doing okay, until the path forks and I have to make a decision. Do I go left or right? I take a guess and follow the path to the left around a building, but it's obviously the wrong guess, because after a minute or two I'm dead-ended at a back door, looking at three enormous garbage bins. Luckily, a couple of kindhearted janitors are taking a break and point me in the right direction.

I run and stumble and walk, and then I start to weave around again, like Coach said I shouldn't do, but I can't help it. I keep going, hoping I'm not lost, hoping I'm not going to collapse or end up with the garbage bins again, hoping that this will all be over soon. It seems like I've been running all day and it feels like the longest day of my life.

At last, I come to the building where Sammy and Wes went to find a bathroom. I follow the trail around the back, half walking, half stumbling, and when I come around the other side, finally, I see the field where we started and the finish line. I'm barely walking now, gasping for air, gripping my side, which, fruit salad or no fruit salad, is in a monstrous stitch. This has all been a disaster.

Coach T is waiting at the finish, holding up her hand for a high five, but I don't even have the energy for a low three. I guess the ref has been waiting for me to finish, because I hear the impatience in his voice when he calls out, "All right, ladies! Let's move this thing along. Three minutes to the gun!"

I barely make it to a nearby tree by the time the ref yells, "Ready!" I plunk down, put my elbows on my knees, and press my hands to my ears as hard as I can. I hear him say, "Set . . ."

BLAM!!!

Sammy, Wes, Mark, and Sanjit are calling out, "Go, Lakeview!" and even from here I can see that Heather is in the lead. She glides along, like a different kind of creature, all long legs and flying hair and determination.

Coach T comes over with a cup of Gatorade. "You finished!" she says.

"But I was terrible," I answer. I'm still trembling from the run, not to mention the girls' starting gun.

Coach T transforms into Mrs. T right before my eyes. She touches my shoulder in that way she does in the Resource Room. "I should've warned you about the gun. That was my fault. We'll take care of it next time. It's an easy fix."

And what would that be, I wonder? A nervous system transplant?

"But you finished," she says again. "You did it. I'm proud of you." Then she gets up and looks at her watch. "I want to be at the finish for the girls. I'll see you over there." She pats me on the back and walks away. I'm glad she doesn't see the Gatorade splatter all over my shorts.

I practically crawl to the finish line, but I get there just in time to add my pathetic "Yay" to the other cheers. Heather finishes first, by a lot. She flashes through the finish tape and takes a few long steps before she comes to a stop.

The rest of the girls come in one by one. They don't look great, but nobody looks as bad as I feel.

When we pile back onto the bus, Victoria says, "That was brutal."

"Are you kidding?" says Sanjit. "It was awesome."

Sammy mumbles, "You didn't have your mother chasing you with a pair of tighty-whities." The girls giggle.

"I'm eating like five bags of chips when I get home," says Wes.

"Ten," says Mark.

As the bus heads back to Lakeview, Coach T turns around. "I want you to know that I'm very proud of you guys," she says. "You all did a fantastic job."

I'm waiting for someone to say, "Except Joseph. Joseph was terrible." But no one does.

Coach T goes on, "Our first meet, and we had a first-place finisher!" Heather ducks and smiles as cheers of "HeathER" fill the bus, and Erica reaches over to give her shoulder a little pat. "But what I'm most proud of," Coach goes on, "is that everybody finished. Every single one of you!"

She's looking at me, but I shrug. I don't feel victorious at all.

As the bus bumps along, I think it all through. I thought I had the worry bases covered: what I ate, staying on the course, wearing this teensy little uniform. I never thought about a gun. And next time there will be something else I never thought of. And the next, and the next.

I realize that my worrying fell short, and it always will, because of a simple rule. I call it the Friedman Law of Worry:

There will always be something you don't think of. And that's what will get you.

So, if the law holds true, maybe I should stop worrying altogether. Or maybe I should vastly expand my worrying categories.

I'm a little unclear which path to take. But then Coach T calls out, "Now, everybody, rest up. Have plenty to drink, and I'll see you at practice tomorrow. Remember, the JFK meet is next week."

So we do all this again in a week.

I better get started on a new worry list tonight.

CHAPTER 18

WHEN I GET HOME, I GO STRAIGHT TO THE kitchen. There's still about an hour before my parents get home. I take a piece of bread and spread it with peanut butter about an inch thick. Then I take some walnuts and press a few into the peanut butter and glob on some of this maple cream that we bought in Vermont this summer, and then I remember that stitch in my side and slice up a banana and put that on there, too. Then I cover the whole thing with another slice of bread. I don't have the patience to sit down to eat it. I just stand at the counter and take a bite.

My mouth is full of peanut butter maple walnut banana sandwich when Grandpa comes in. "So, how was it?" he asks. "Did you win?"

I give him a squinty look and shake my head.

"But you didn't quit?" I shrug and shake my head. "That's my boy." I brace for a back slap, but Grandpa just rumples my hair instead. "Eat your snack. I've got some Web surfing to do," he says and goes back to the guest bedroom.

I pour myself a glass of orange juice and drink it in about

five gulps. I take a quick shower, then go to my room and change into my regular clothes. I flop down on the bed and my mind flies in a million directions. I replay the start of the race, the gun, the garbage bins, all of it. I keep hearing Coach T's words: "You did it. I'm proud of you." And Grandpa's: "You didn't quit? That's my boy."

I'm glad they're both proud of me. I really am. But I have to wonder, Does not quitting lead to something better, like actually accomplishing something? Or is just not quitting going to be my goal forever?

I know that Grandpa is a big fan of not quitting. I remember once in second grade when he took me to basketball practice. It was a Saturday morning. I guess my parents were away, probably at a dental equipment conference, because Grandpa drove me over to the Griffith Elementary School gym.

I was seven and I loved the gym. I couldn't get over how shiny the floor was, like someone had poured liquid glass all over it. Under the polish was golden wood with bright-colored lines that had mysterious meanings I'd never understand. I loved the shrieks my sneakers made when I ran. I couldn't stop tiny-stepping around so I could hear it over and over. "Eek-eek-eek. Eek-eek-eek."

My gym teacher didn't love any of that, especially while he was trying to talk.

"Joseph! Stand still! Joseph!" Mr. Hensarling would say. And when I didn't stop, "Friedman! Enough!"

I guess that's when it started. The Friedman thing.

But Mr. Hensarling wasn't there for weekend rec. On Saturdays, second-grade rec basketball was run by Sean Maurer's dad. His favorite word was DE-fense. "DE-fense! DE-fense wins games! DE-fense is what makes a good team GREAT!"

He showed us how to play DE-fense—get in front of the kid with the ball, jump up high, wave your arms like a maniac. I thought I was pretty good at it, actually. I jumped, I waved, I even made funny faces. So I didn't understand why Sean's dad came marching over to me.

"Joseph," he said, trying to force his face into a smile. "You play defense against the other team. Michael's on your team. You don't play defense against him."

"Oh," I said. I wished he'd explained that before.

Everything about second-grade basketball was harder than first grade. In first grade, we had fun drills: bouncing, passing, trying to shoot for the basket. Casey Minter's dad ran those clinics, and he cheered for everybody, even if we missed a hundred times or dropped the ball. He didn't mind if I decided to run around in circles, making my sneakers squeal.

But Sean Maurer's dad was serious. He had a whistle around his neck. A terrible, screaming whistle. And he wore cowboy boots, which wouldn't even be allowed if Mr. Hensarling was in charge.

Sean's dad put us in teams. Suddenly there were certain kids who were on your side and others who weren't. It seemed like every two seconds everyone reversed course and ran the other way. It didn't seem hard for Sean and his friends. Sean could even dribble the ball with one hand and motion some kind of directions to his friend Julian with the other. But I kept getting it wrong. It was so confusing. I stopped hoping that I'd get the ball and make a basket, and started hoping that I wouldn't be noticed and I'd never have to touch the ball, ever again.

So that one morning when I heard Sean's dad yelling, "Joseph! Back on D! Back on D!" all I could think was *What's D? And why is he so mad?* I stopped and turned and that was when Daniel Showalter crashed into me. And I found out that you can slide pretty far on those shiny gym floors—all the way to the bleachers, where I crashed into, and sort of under, the bottom one.

Everybody stopped and looked over. I just stayed where I was, all crunched up, half under that bleacher, and I remember thinking that second grade is when sports aren't fun anymore.

Sean's dad blew the whistle again and the game stopped and he came over and peered down at me. "You okay?"

I nodded.

"Your parents here?"

"I'm with him," said my grandpa. From my position on the floor, he looked big. Bigger even than Sean's dad. "Go back to your game, cowboy."

Sean's dad didn't answer. He blew the whistle, which shrieked in my ears, and motioned for all the kids to get back on the court.

Grandpa was scratching his head and smiling down at me. I guess I looked comfortable enough under there.

"What are you doing down there, Superhero?" He called me that even back then. It went back to when I was about three and insisted on wearing my Batman costume out to dinner.

"I slid," I answered. He put out his hand and pulled me up. "Can we go?" I asked.

Grandpa shook his head. "You should sit back down with the team."

"I don't like basketball," I said.

"I know," said Grandpa. He was brushing the dust off my shorts. "Go sit next to Mr. Ball Hog there." He motioned toward Sean.

"I don't want to."

"I don't blame you," said Grandpa.

"What did you call him?"

"A ball hog. He doesn't pass the ball. And you won't have

to sit next to him long. His dad's going to put him back in the game."

"Can't we just go home?" I asked.

"The right thing to do is stay. You're on a team, and quitting isn't a good habit."

I listened to Grandpa and went to sit next to Sean. Grandpa was right. He went right back into the game.

I never got any better at basketball, but it wasn't so bad, because after a while, Sean's dad pretty much left me on the bench. I could just sit and listen to everybody else's sneakers squeak, and cover my ears when the whistle blew.

The problem with cross country is there's no bench. There's no hiding and there's no way to be bad enough that they tell you to sit down and watch.

At least there's the possibility of a PR. Today was so bad, it would be hard to get worse. Then again, if anybody could, it would be me. Maybe one day I'll have a bigger goal, like actually being good at something. But I don't see it happening anytime soon. For now, I'll settle for not quitting. I think it's about all the challenge I can handle.

CHAPTER 19

SCIENCE IS USUALLY ONE OF MY BETTER CLASSES. Wes is in it and so is Heather. Heather sits behind me, which is helpful because she clears her throat or kicks my chair when she sees that my attention is wandering. Also, there are labs at least once a week, so instead of just listening and writing stuff down, we can combine things in tubes and hope they explode.

It's Wednesday, and Mr. Hoolihan is late. Most of the kids are talking, sitting on the desks, and putting their feet on the chairs. A kid named Cody is keeping watch while Wes tries to open Mr. Hoolihan's bottom desk drawer, to see if it's true that he keeps a bottle of whiskey in there.

My desk is in the front row, by the door. Heather is in her seat behind me and she's doodling in her notebook.

That's when Charlie Kastner walks by. First he sees Cody. Then he sees Wes fiddling with Mr. Hoolihan's desk. I guess it looks interesting, so he saunters in.

Then he sees me.

NEWS FLASH to seventh-grade teachers: When you're late, bad things happen.

Charlie sits himself down on my desk. It's not that big a desk. He fans himself with the flimsy hall pass that he's somehow wrangled from one of his teachers. There's a shredded hole in his jeans and a piece of blubbery thigh is poking through.

"So, Friedman," he says, shifting to make himself comfortable, "you're having some trouble with the starting gun, huh? I hear it makes you cry like a little girl."

I don't look up. Maybe I can wait him out. Mr. Hoolihan will be here soon. He's got to be. "Too bad, Friedman," says Charlie. "I thought a sissy sport like track would be just right for you." He wiggles his fingers when he says "track," like he's sprinkling fairy dust or something. "I bet that's what they told you in the Retards . . . I mean Resource Room."

Wes is still crouched down behind Mr. Hoolihan's desk. I know he hears Charlie, but he stays where he is. I don't blame him.

"Maybe it's time to try cheerleading," Charlie goes on. "You thought about that? Or hockey? You can be the puck. Yeah, that's an idea. You can be the PUCK." He says "PUCK" really loud and right in my face, spraying me with spit.

"We're running cross country. And it isn't a sissy sport," says Heather. She's still sitting at her desk.

Charlie looks at Heather and stands up. He's like a drooling hyena about to pounce on a field mouse when he suddenly catches sight of a nice, juicy zebra. He faces Heather and leans on her desk with a slanty grin. "Yeah? It's not a sissy sport? You think Friedman here could play football, huh?"

Heather stands up, too. She leans on her side of the desk and they're practically nose to nose. She's taking Charlie on, just like she did that day in soccer. I'm shaking my head at her vigorously and praying that Mr. Hoolihan will come in and send Charlie back to wherever he's supposed to be.

"Why would he want to?" she says. "The football team stinks."

Now Charlie straightens up. "What did you say?"

"I said, your team stinks. Fairfield kicked your butts last week, your front line is weak right to left, and they're running through your defense like you're a bunch of old ladies. You're oh-and-three. So maybe you should just shut up about who's the sissy."

It's totally quiet in the room. Wes's mouth is hanging open. Everybody's watching Charlie and Heather to see what will happen next.

Charlie is quiet for a few seconds, but then he gets a different kind of grin on his face. More like a sneer. "You've hurt my feelings," he says. "I think I'll go tell my mom." I don't know what he's getting at. Heather keeps staring and doesn't move. "My mom loves me a lot. She comes to all my games to cheer for me. Too bad yours isn't around—"

I hardly know what's happened, but all of a sudden Charlie Kastner is on the floor. I look at Heather and Heather's face and Heather's fist and realize that she's punched him. Hard.

That's when Mr. Hoolihan makes his entrance. It isn't difficult for him to figure out what happened with Charlie screaming, "She punched me! She punched me in the nose!" Besides, there are also about twenty witnesses. Heather looks like if Charlie took a step toward her she would punch him again, but Charlie is too busy bleeding all over the place to even try.

Chairs are screeching as everybody backs away from the fight scene. I don't know if it's to avoid getting mixed up in the trouble or because nobody wants to get splattered with the blood that's pouring out of Charlie's nose.

There's a sink in the science room and a pile of those brown paper towels that seem to repel more liquid than they soak up. Mr. Hoolihan bunches up a handful and hands them to Charlie, but the blood pretty much bypasses them and drips all over the floor.

"Frank," says Mr. Hoolihan, "take him to the nurse." He hands Frank some more paper towels. I almost laugh at Frank's face as he looks from the wad of towels to Charlie's spurting nose.

Charlie stumbles up and out the door and Frank follows him. Then Mr. Hoolihan tells Heather to go to the principal.

He really has no choice. She doesn't argue, she just heads straight for the door without looking at anybody. Maybe I'm imagining it, but I think somebody's cheering for her from the back of the room.

Once they're gone, Mr. Hoolihan covers the blood on the floor with about six inches of paper towels. He tries to get us to focus on the difference between igneous and sedimentary rocks, but it's like the whole class has ADD. Everybody's talking and whispering. As soon as one corner of the room stops, another corner starts.

My mind is jumping all over the place: I'm hoping that Heather isn't in too much trouble. I'm wondering how Charlie knew about the starting gun. I'm thinking that whatever he said must have hurt her really badly. Mostly, I'm trying to imagine what it would feel like to have the courage to do what Heather did.

Behind me, I hear Wes's voice. I guess he's thinking the same thing. "That," he says, "was awesome."

CHAPTER 20

HEATHER ISN'T IN SCHOOL THE NEXT DAY. THE word is that she's been suspended. Charlie isn't in school, either. The word is that he's black and blue and suspended. I've never known a suspended person. Now I know two.

I feel at least partly to blame. If I'd been able to stand up for myself, Heather wouldn't have gotten involved, she wouldn't have punched Charlie, and today she'd be running in the JFK meet with the rest of the team.

It rained last night, the kind of rain that drums on the roof and pulls the leaves off the trees and makes my mom say she's glad we don't have a dog. When the rain slowed down, a blast of cold air came in, like instant winter. It's still misting a little and now we're glad we have our gigantic Lakeview Leopards sweats.

As the bus pulls up, Wes and Sammy are dueling with their oversize sweatshirt arms, swatting each other with the cuffs. Mark grabs the ends of Sanjit's sleeves and crosses and pulls them behind him, so Sanjit's arms are wrapped around his body.

"Take me to your leader," says Sanjit, and Mark leads him onto the bus.

The rest of the boys follow and then the girls. We take seats and wait for Coach T. I'm sitting by myself.

"It's not fair that Heather has to miss the meet," says Sammy.

It's not like I was thinking about Heather, exactly, but it's one of those times when I have a general feeling that something's wrong, and as soon as I hear her name, I realize that's what it is.

"Yeah, and Charlie gets to play," says Mark.

"What?" says Sanjit, wriggling his sleeves free. "How does that work?"

"Charlie's game is on Saturday so his suspension is up," says Mark.

"That's not fair," says Erica. She was sitting toward the back, but now she moves up to join the conversation.

"What started it, anyway?" asks Brianne.

Wes scoots up in his seat, ready to tell everything. "Well, first, Charlie was giving Joseph a hard time about the starting gun," he says.

There it is, I'm thinking. It's all my fault. Now everybody's going to hate me and blame me for everything. But instead, Sanjit just says, "What a lowlife," and the others all start talking over each other.

"How did he know?" asks Teresa.

"Yeah, who even told him about that?" says Brianne.

"We were the only ones there," says Sammy.

Then I hear a little squeak from Victoria. She's been quiet all this time, her chin tucked into her chest, her arms folded, with about two feet of extra sweatshirt arm drooping on either side of her. She adds a sniff to the squeak and then a frown and then she picks up her elbows and digs them back down into her body and says, "It was me."

Suddenly, all the talking stops and everybody's looking at Victoria. "I was so stupid," she says, and she's starting to cry. "Charlie was with Zachary and Zachary's so cute and everything."

"*Muy guapo*," says Teresa, nodding. Sammy scowls.

"They asked me how the meet went and I said okay. Then they asked me how Heather did and how Joseph did and I told them what happened with the starting gun. I knew when I said it I shouldn't have." Victoria is wiping her eyes with the two feet of extra sweatshirt sleeve and Teresa is patting her on the shoulder. "I'm really sorry, Joseph," says Victoria, turning to me. "I didn't mean to make fun of you, it was just kind of funny and I didn't think . . ."

"It's okay," I say, because I've been made fun of about ten thousand times, but this is the first time ever that anybody's apologized. "Really. It's okay."

"I'm never talking to those idiots again," says Victoria. All the girls nod. So does Sammy.

"So, then what happened?" asks Mark. "With Heather and Charlie?"

"Then he started saying something about Heather's mom," says Wes.

"Her mom?" repeats Teresa.

"Something about her not being around."

Now everybody starts talking over each other again.

"That's mean," says Sanjit.

"Her mom's not here?" asks Erica.

"That's so sad," says Brianne.

"Maybe something happened to her," says Mark.

"Poor Heather," adds Erica.

As they all talk, I'm mad at myself all over again. Why didn't I ever ask her? It was right there on her emergency sheet, and I never said anything. And why didn't I stand up to Charlie? None of this would've happened if it wasn't for me.

Everybody's talking about Heather and Charlie and guessing about Heather's mother, until Coach T steps onto the bus and everything gets quiet. "Everybody okay?" she asks. We nod in unison and she looks around, a little puzzled, but then she says, "Then fasten your seatbelts. We're off to JFK."

As we bump along, Victoria frees her hand from her sleeve and wipes her last tear with a flick of her ring finger. Sanjit turns around to face me. "Have you talked to her?"

"Who?"

"Heather."

"No," I say. "Why?"

"Because, you're, like, friends, right?"

The word takes me by surprise. "Sort of," I say. If I am, I must be a really bad one. The kind who doesn't ask about something as big as not having your mother around. The kind who lets somebody else fight his battles.

I guess I'm looking pretty glum, because after a couple of minutes, Coach T comes over and sits next to me. "Joseph," she says.

"Coach T," I answer.

"How are you?"

"I'm fine," I say. "How are you?"

"I'm a little sad about Heather," she says. "I wish she were here."

I nod. "Me, too."

She puts her hand on my shoulder. "Will you be able to concentrate on the race? Do you think you can do that?"

It's not an easy question. My mind doesn't always cooperate when I try to keep it on one thing.

"Can you try?"

"Yes," I say, because that's an easier question.

Then Coach reaches into her pocket and pulls something out. "You know, Heather and I talked about you, after the last race."

"You did?"

"We both had the same idea. Something that might help you with the starting gun. Here." She hands me a packet of squishy little pillows. They're shaped like bullets and they're a light green color that I don't quite trust.

"They're earplugs," she says, in case I hadn't figured it out.

I stare at them and squeeze the package a few times. I think about the starting gun and flinch a little, just remembering it. I feel funny, though—kind of guilty. "Is this cheating?" I ask Coach.

"Why?"

"Because nobody else is using them."

"Nobody else needs them," she answers. "If they did, they could use them, too." She gives me another tap on the shoulder, and goes back to her seat.

I open the package and try putting one in my ear. It pops out and lands in the grubby rubberized bus aisle. I take out another one and try again, and again the puffy little pellet pops out.

"My brother plays in a band and my dad makes him use those," says Brianne, who's a couple seats away. "You have to push them way in."

I put one in each ear and push hard.

Brianne keeps talking, but her voice sounds tiny now. It's like I'm hearing her through a marshmallow. "My little sister found one and put it up her nose and my mom had to use tweezers to get it out."

"Wow," I say, and I scare myself, because it sounds like I'm yelling into my own ears.

I pull the plugs out and it's like coming up from underwater. The bus engine roars and everyone's voices clang in my ears. Then the bus bounces around a corner and turns in to the JFK driveway.

"I've got to pee," says Wes to nobody in particular as the bus sighs to a stop.

"Later, Wes," says Coach T, looking at her watch. "You need to walk the course. Go. Go!" We all pile out and there's a JFK kid who's waiting to show us the course. We follow him to the starting line, which is around the school building, across a field, and up some stairs. Then he shows us the course, which is mostly through the woods. It's still wet from last night's rain, and the trees drip cold water on our heads and shoulders. I stay to the side of the trail and use the tree roots like stepping-stones. After the woods there's a paved walkway that we'll run to get to the finish. I check for worms, but the path seems clear.

When we get back to the starting line, the ref calls out, "Girls' race is first! Line up, ladies!"

By now Wes is jumping from leg to leg. "Hey, JFK kid," he says, "where's the bathroom?"

"Dude, it's all the way back where the bus let you off," he says. "You should've gone then."

"You somebody's mother or something?" says Mark.

"Can't you hold it in?" I ask.

"I had two Arnies," he answers, "and a Gatorade."

"Two whats?" asks Mark.

"Arnold Palmers. Half lemonade, half iced tea. Oh, man, saying it makes it worse. I've got to go." Wes looks around and starts off for the woods.

"Wait! The girls are coming through there in like a minute . . ." Mark says, but Wes has already disappeared into the trees.

The girls have left their sweats in a pile, and they're lined up at the start, shivering in their uniforms.

"Ready . . ." says the ref. I fumble with my earplugs and stuff them in.

"Set . . ." *Blam.* I hear the shot, but it's like it's wrapped in cotton. I don't even jump. I wish Heather was here to witness my victory, but then again, if she was here, she wouldn't be looking at me. She'd be at the starting line, darting ahead of the pack.

I take the earplugs out, and even though my hearing is sharp and clear now, once the girls' footsteps fade out, everything is still and quiet.

Sanjit is stretching. Sammy and Mark are trying to do handstands. I think about Heather, and what Sanjit said. About us being friends. I guess that's how it looks from the outside. Maybe it's how it is on the inside, too. I'm not sure.

While the girls run, I spend some time squishing my earplugs, watching them flatten and pop back into form. I try to remember what Coach T asked me to do: Focus on the race. See the course in my mind. Get ready to run.

After about fifteen minutes, one of the girls comes out of the woods and starts down the flagged-off finish lane. From where we stand, she looks like she's wearing boots, but then I realize it's mud, from her shoes up to her knees. All the girls behind her have mud on their legs too, and splattered on their uniforms. The last of them are half running, half walking, looking down and trying to brush spots of mud off their shorts with quick little strokes.

When all the girls have crossed the finish line, the ref calls out, "Okay, boys, let's go."

We throw off our sweats and line up. Wes pushes in between Sammy and me.

"Feel better?" asks Sammy.

"Yeah," he says. He seems more cheerful.

"Did the girls see you?"

"Yeah. I was like ten yards off the trail."

"What did you do?" Sanjit asks.

"I called, 'Go Lakeview!'"

The ref calls, "Up to the line, gentlemen! Two minutes to the gun!"

As I stuff the earplugs in, a heavy kid in a Fox Ridge singlet lines up on my left. "Watch out going into the woods," he mutters. "It's the Wild West out there."

I'm not sure if I should say thanks, but it doesn't matter because the ref calls, "One minute!" and I press my fingers into my ears, pushing the earplugs in deep.

"Ready. Set . . ." *Blam.* The gunshot is cotton-wrapped again. I breathe a sigh of relief and relax. The only thing is, I forget to move.

"Go, son," says the ref in a cloudy voice. "Go on. Run!"

"Oh! Thanks," I say as I start out running, zigzagging across the field because I'm trying to get the earplugs out.

Up ahead, all the runners are crunched up together, trying to get onto the woods trail. I can see what that kid was talking about. Elbows are flying and there's pushing and shoving as kids jockey for position. By the time I go into the woods, there's only that Fox Ridge kid and me left, and we practically fall over ourselves to let the other go first.

In the woods, the trail is a river of mud. It's drizzling and the ground is slippery and wet and just overall disgusting. The roots and rocks and dry patches I used to keep my balance in the walk-through are long gone, drowned in mud. With every step it splatters my uniform, my legs, even my face, but it's no use wiping it off, because all I see in front of me is mud and more mud.

The Fox Ridge kid has fallen back, but now he's lumbering up behind me. I think he must have tripped somewhere along the way. He's covered with mud. It kind of looks like he's fallen into a vat of hot fudge.

I raise my hand to let him know that I know he's there, that I share his pain. It's kind of a comfort, sharing the trail with him, and we slog along, half running, half walking, for what seems like hours, sliding and sloshing through puddles, until we finally reach the end of the woods. By now the paved path is muddy and slick, so we both slow down even more.

As I see the finish line in the distance, the Fox Ridge kid pulls up next to me.

"I'm Heber," he pants.

"Joseph," I say, thinking, *Boy, some kids just can't catch a break.*

"Get ready for the pity cheer," he says.

"The what?"

"The pity cheer. You'll see."

As we reach the last stretch I see a bunch of mothers with looks on their faces like they're watching videos of cats and puppies slipping and sliding across a waxed floor—sort of a mixture of sad and funny. I guess he has it right. It's pity.

"Attaway," says a guy with a whistle. We walk for a few seconds, then try to run again.

"Now somebody's gonna say, 'Lookin' good,'" Heber says.

"How do you—"

"Lookin' good!" a stranger calls out.

"See? The pity cheer. Now go ahead. I can't keep up." Heber falls back a few steps and I manage to stumble across the line to a smattering of applause.

Heber finishes behind me. "See you next time," he says, then bumbles away.

When we finally climb back onto the bus, we look like we've been in a Civil War battle. As the bus starts up, Coach says, "Now, everybody, did you see how Joseph was running with that boy from Fox Ridge? It's a good lesson for everyone."

"That no matter how pathetic we are, there's someone more pathetic?" suggests Sammy.

"No, Sammy. That we can all work to help each other. Even on different teams, we can support one another."

"I like what Sammy said better," says Wes.

Teresa taps Wes on the shoulder. "That was really nice of you, to go into the woods to cheer for us."

"Yeah, thanks, Wes," says Victoria.

Sammy frowns when Victoria sits down next to Wes. Mark claps a hand over his mouth to keep from laughing.

"Oh, hey, it was nothing," says a smiling Wes. "Anything to support the team."

CHAPTER 21

I'VE NEVER BEEN TO A GIRL'S HOUSE. WELL, maybe not never, but never since about first grade. I know I've never been to a girl's house after she was suspended. And I've absolutely never been to a girl's house after she was suspended for punching a guy because of me.

But Coach T ended practice early—I guess as a reward for surviving yesterday's Mud Meet—and instead of going home, I find myself walking down Underhill Avenue to Heather's house. Underhill is a windy road that splits Lakeview into two jigsaw-puzzle-ish pieces. There are no sidewalks, just a strip of dirt and grass. It's still raining a little, and every car that goes by sends a splattery fountain of muddy water right at me.

On this side of Lakeview, most of the houses are big and stony. They have curving driveways with crunchy gray gravel. One house has a tennis court and a pool with a water slide. I can see the slide's shiny handles peeking out over the fence. But Heather's house is small and skinny. It's pinky tan, with brown windowsills. It blends in perfectly with the fallen leaves, like it's trying not to be noticed.

There's a tall chain-link fence separating Heather's back-yard from Cloverdale Golf Club. Cloverdale's lawn is still a rich autumn green, and its clubhouse is perched on a velvety hill, peering down in an I'm-better-than-you way. I wonder if maybe that's what Heather's house is hiding from.

There's a short cement walk leading to Heather's front door. I stand at the end of it and stare. I feel stupid. I should have called. I should have texted. I should have done any-thing but wander over here like this, not knowing if Heather is mad at me or upset or thinking that I'm the most pathetic coward she's ever met and this is all my fault.

I'm about to turn back when the door opens. Heather is talking on her cell, but she waves me in, like I come over ev-ery day.

"I know that," she's saying into the phone. "Don't worry. I'm not going to punch anybody else out."

I *squish squish* my way through the soggy leaves to the front door. I leave my muddy shoes on the rug by the door, even though it doesn't seem like the kind of house where there are rules about stuff like that. It's more of a tromp-right-in-and-throw-your-coat-on-the-banister kind of house.

There's a high-pitched whistle coming from somewhere, and Heather motions for me to follow her down a short hallway. In the kitchen, steam is streaming from a blue teakettle. Heather puts her phone on speaker and drops it on the counter to free up her hands. Then she moves the kettle to another burner and turns the knob off.

When the whistle stops, a woman's voice fills the room.

"You should see the flora here!" the voice is saying. "It's just extraordinary!"

Heather opens a cabinet and shuffles some cereal boxes around, looking for something. I wonder what a flora is. The voice continues, "There's one flower, the *Hibiscus waimeae*. It lasts for only a single day. A single day! Each one starts out white and fades to pink in the afternoon. Oh, honey, I'm just in love with it."

"Mom—" Heather says, and my heart does a little jump.

I guess her mom doesn't hear her, because she just keeps talking. "There are chickens running loose everywhere," she says, laughing. "And roosters! They jump up on the table and stare me down when I'm eating on the terrace. And the orchids! All the colors, the fragrances. You know they filmed *Jurassic Park* here. And *South Pacific*! There are rainbows every day, and there's a little village called Hanalei—"

"Mom," says Heather again, a little louder. She grabs a box of Swiss Miss hot chocolate and puts it on the counter.

"—Hanalei! Like in 'Puff, the Magic Dragon'!"

"Mom, I don't even know . . ."

Then Heather's mom starts singing, although it's more like the phone on the counter starts singing, "Puff the Magic

141

Dra-a-a-a-g-on lived by the sea, and frolicked in the autumn mist, in a land called Hana-le-e-e-e-e-e-e . . ."

Heather shoots me a glance and reaches for the phone, but not before I hear her mother say, "I'm just so in love with this place, Heather, I can't bear to—"

"Mom!" shouts Heather, taking it off speaker. "Please, stop. It sounds great. Really. It sounds beautiful, but . . ." She looks at me again. "Somebody's here and I have to go." She listens for a second. "A kid from the team."

She listens some more. "One meet. Yeah, I won." Her mom talks some more, then finally Heather says, "Okay, but I doubt . . ." And then, "Of course. I will. I promise. Okay. Okay. Yeah, me too. Bye."

She hangs up, and before I can say anything, she looks me over and says, "What happened to you?" I look down. I could be a Tide commercial.

"Mud," I say with a shrug.

"Have some hot chocolate," she says. "You can spill it all over yourself and nobody could even tell." I nod, and she turns to pull two mugs from a shelf I'd need a stepstool to reach.

While her back is turned, I say, "I came to tell you I'm sorry."

"Why?" she asks, without turning around.

"Because if I'd stood up to Charlie then he wouldn't have

said what he said and you wouldn't have hit him and they wouldn't have suspended you and you wouldn't have missed the meet yesterday and you wouldn't be mad at me."

She turns around and waggles two Swiss Miss packets, shaking down the powder so it doesn't explode all over the place like it does when I open packets of Swiss Miss.

"I'm not mad at you," she says.

"You're not?"

"No. For one thing, I got to meet the principal. Definitely a manatee, by the way," she says, puffing her cheeks and lips into what I guess must be a manatee face. "And besides, I'm kind of glad it's out of the way." She rips the tops off the packets and pours the cocoa powder and hot water into the mugs. "Charlie was going to say something eventually. It was just a matter of time. I know he hears them over at Cloverdale, saying all sorts of things that aren't true. Like my mom doesn't care about me. Like she's not coming back."

She puts the mugs down on the painted yellow table, drops a spoon in each, and we both sit down.

"Where is she?" I ask.

"Hawaii. 'The land of Hanalei,'" she adds, shaking her head.

"Wow. That's far." I'm not sure what else to say, so I concentrate on smushing up a clump of cocoa powder with my spoon.

"She's writing a paper on some endangered flowers. She's a botanist."

"Like your dad?"

"Well, almost. He's a horticulturist. He grows plants, my mom studies them. That's how he describes it. They met because of Furbish's lousewort."

"Furb what?"

"Furbish's lousewort. It's a plant that someone found growing on a riverbank in Maine. It was supposed to be extinct, so it was a really big deal to find it there." Heather gets up, takes a small picture off the refrigerator door and hands it to me. I guess it's her mom and dad. And the Furbish's lousewort. The plant looks like an asparagus with little yellow flowers, nothing special at all. In fact, it's pretty ugly. Her dad looks young and skinny and her mom looks really pretty.

"Anyway," says Heather, "my mom went to Hawaii and she was supposed to be finished in a couple of weeks, but now it's been like a month and . . ." She shrugs and points to the phone, like what I heard is all she knows. "My dad says you can find fascinating things right where you are if you just look hard enough. But my mom . . ."

Heather stares into her hot chocolate. I stare into mine. I have a vision of the two of us sitting here in hot-cocoa silence for the next hour. But then I remember how bad I felt that I never asked Heather anything about her mom. I don't want to say the wrong thing, but saying nothing doesn't seem right. Then I think, *If I was Heather, what would I want a friend to say?*

Finally, I ask, "Do you miss her a lot?"

Heather nods. "I guess I should be used to it. When I was ten, she went to New Mexico for a month to study some rare cactus. Before that was a parrot flower somewhere in Thailand. And then there were these pitcher plants somewhere that eat frogs."

"The plants? Eat frogs?"

Heather nods. "And large insects. Sometimes mice."

Well, I think, at least it's good to know in advance what my nightmares will be tonight.

"And when she's home, it's kind of like she's just planning her next time away." Heather takes the picture and puts it back on the fridge. Then she comes back to the table. "She sends me neat stuff, though. I have this feathery charm from New Mexico and a jeweled elephant from Thailand. And she's sending me a sarong from Hawaii."

"What's a sarong?"

"A long dress-thing," she says, "with flowers."

"Oh," I say. I try picturing Heather in a long, flowery dress. It doesn't seem quite right, but then again, it took me a while to get used to Mrs. T in sweatpants.

"I guess she thinks I'm a Blueberry Princess like her,

not someone who goes around punching football players." Heather gives a one-shouldered shrug. "Maybe if she was around more, she'd know."

"Hey, even a Blueberry Princess would want to punch Charlie," I say, trying to cheer her up. "Everybody thought you were awesome. We couldn't believe the look on Charlie's face when you said the football team stunk."

The corners of her mouth do a little twitch. I think she's trying not to smile.

"Frank told Wes that Charlie was bleeding all the way down the hall and all he had was this little bunch of brown paper towels to wipe it up." Heather shakes her head and covers her mouth. "Nicole Abruzzi was so grossed out she had to go home. And the custodian needed like a gallon of Mr. Clean stuff to clean it. We were all talking about it on the bus to the meet."

Finally, Heather lets herself smile. She scoots her chair back a little, stretches out her long legs, and folds her arms. "So," she asks, "what about the meet?"

"What about the meet?"

She punches me in the arm. "How was it?"

"Muddy," I say.

"Did you PR?"

"Barely. It was like swimming in mud. But I wasn't last. There was this guy named Heber. He was even slower than me."

"Heber?" She looks like she doesn't believe me.

"Yeah. Really."

I tell her about the soft green earplugs and the pity cheer and even Wes's trip to the woods, but I make her swear not to tell the other girls about that. I tell her about Victoria and how she felt so bad for telling Charlie about me and the starting gun. Heather even agrees with the other girls about Zachary being cute, but a creep. I tell her again how the whole team wished she was there and how she would've won by a mile.

Then I hear the front door open, and footsteps coming down the hall. "In here, Dad!" Heather calls.

I don't know what I was expecting. Maybe a mad scientist in a white coat with goggles and a spray gun to battle all the golf course rot and mold Heather told me about that day at the track. But when Heather's dad comes into the kitchen he turns out to be pretty much the same tall, gangly guy I saw in the picture, with a scruffy beard. His hair is in a ponytail and he's wearing a flannel shirt and big work boots.

"Hey," says Heather. "This is Joseph. He's on the cross country team."

"You came by to see the prisoner?" he says, leaning over to give her a kiss on the cheek.

"My suspension is over, Dad," says Heather. "I'm free."

"Well, that's a relief," says her father. "I was getting tired of sliding food under the door. And the noise of that tin cup rattling the bars." I'm happy to see Heather laugh. Her father goes over to the refrigerator. He takes out a can of Mountain Dew, which fits perfectly with the ponytail and flannel.

"Mom called," says Heather. Her dad flips the top of the can, but he doesn't move.

"And?"

"She's sending me a sarong."

"A sarong?"

"It's a dress," I say. "With flowers." After I say it, I realize that he probably already knew that.

"She says she's in love with Hawaii," says Heather.

Heather's dad has that same sad look that Heather had before. I feel like it's up to me to get things going again. I can't think of anything else, so I blurt out, "Are you making progress with the bronze birch borer beetles over at Cloverdale?" Unlike things I'm going to be quizzed on, certain phrases stick in my brain and never leave.

Heather's dad gives a surprised laugh. "How did you know about that?"

"Heather told me. She said you could get rid of them. She said you're an expert."

"She did?" He smiles and moves back behind Heather's chair. "Well, I'd say we have them on the run. We're going to lose a couple of trees. We were too late to save all of them. But I think most will come back healthy in the spring. You can come over to the course sometime and I'll show you."

"Great," I say, although I'm not sure I want to go to a golf club where Charlie is a member.

"Well," says Heather's dad, "I have some paperwork to do. Nice meeting you, Joseph." He reaches across the table and we shake hands. His palm is rough from working and cold from the soda can. He gives me the kind of wink I wish I could master. When I practice in the mirror, I just look like I have something in my eye. He kisses Heather on the head, then touches his nose and pulls on his ear before heading down the hall.

"What was that?" I ask.

"Oh. Baseball signals. He coached my team in Cherry-field. I liked that one. It doesn't mean anything. You just do it to make the other team nervous."

It's really time for me to get home, but first I tell Heather about the French quiz on Tuesday. It's about the verb "to be," which is so confusing it makes me wonder if French people just don't want anybody else speaking their language.

"Want to study for it?" Heather asks. "I can come to your house Monday, after practice."

"Sure," I say, trying to sound like I have friends over all the time. I take a last gulp of hot chocolate, tipping the cup way back to hide my smile. It's the best part, all thick and sweet and muddy.

◆ ◆ ◆

That night when I get into bed, I think about how unfair it is that Heather's mom isn't here. Maybe the rules change when you grow up. Maybe there are times when you can quit, for a while at least. But I don't think you should be allowed to quit on people. And nobody should be allowed to quit on Heather.

It's nice and warm under the covers. It feels good, being home, listening to the rain outside. My muscles ache, from the meet, from practice, from my run home from Heather's. I didn't mean to run. It started as a walk, but soon I was going faster. I was thinking about what Heather told her dad, "She says she's in love with Hawaii," and I dug my sneakers harder into the dirt. I heard Charlie's voice, "My mom loves me a lot," and I kicked at the stones by the road. I pushed against the ground and my thighs clenched and my arms pumped. It hurt, but it also felt good, in a way I've never felt before.

My mom comes in and sits on the bed next to me. I can't imagine her not here with me and my dad. If she wants to go to Thailand, she doesn't say so. There must be times when things aren't what she expected, when I'm not what she expected, but if there are, she's never let me know.

My arm wants to hug her, but I don't let it because she'd get all worried, with me suddenly hugging her like a four-year-old. So I just sort of stiffen my arm muscle around her and bury my face in the pillow, sort of like a silent hug. I don't think she notices anything different from usual.

But when she turns out the light and kisses the top of my head, I say, "Mom? Do you and Dad want to see me run?"

She stops in the doorway and says, "Of course we do!"

"The last meet is at Lakeview. It's the league championship. If you want to come, it's okay."

She comes back and sits on my bed and gently pushes the hair back off my forehead. "You sure we won't make you too nervous? You won't get distracted and run into a tree?"

I know she's joking, but that is actually a possibility.

"I'll try not to," I say.

"Then we'll be there."

"And Mom," I add, "remember that girl I told you about? The one who beat Charlie in soccer that day? Her name is Heather. Can you cheer for her, too?"

Her hand pauses on top of my head, just for a second. I can feel her curiosity glowing through the darkness.

"She's new, and her mom is away," I explain.

I hear her take a breath, like she's about to ask something else, but then she doesn't. She just kisses me again and says, "Of course. Just point her out to me."

"Oh, I won't have to," I say. "You'll know. She'll be the fastest one there."

CHAPTER 22

I HAVEN'T HAD VERY GOOD LUCK BEING FRIENDS. When I was little, my parents made play dates for me, but my mom had to drive me because I cried if somebody else's mom picked me up. At Jayden Probst's house, the babysitter gave us a snack called ants on a log without telling me that they weren't real ants. I hid in the bathroom until she promised they were gone. And Liam McFarrin wouldn't let me use any of his new crayons. He gave me a separate box and they were all broken, with about eight blues and no reds at all.

By the time I was seven or eight, school days seemed to last forever. Play dates felt like more homework—one more thing that always came out wrong. I hated going to some kid's house just so he could cream me at video games or trounce me at baseball.

But who knows? Maybe things have changed.

I try to picture my house the way Heather will see it when she comes over: the pictures of my family, my mother's little Post-it note reminders all over the refrigerator.

And Grandpa.

I love Grandpa, but what if he says something embarrassing? What if he says I'm afraid of lima beans or tells her about the time I ran away from Mr. Peanut in the mall? What if he calls me Superhero or asks her how she got so tall?

So, on Monday morning, I decide to head him off at the pass. "Grandpa," I say in my most casual voice, "a friend of mine is coming over after school to study with me. She's in my French class."

His eyebrows go up and he says, "A girlfriend?" Just what I was afraid of.

"No," I answer. I try to sound firm and not amused. "She's just someone in my French class."

"She's smart?" he asks.

I nod. "Especially in French. And she's on the cross country team. She's a really good runner."

"So she likes you," says Grandpa.

"She doesn't like me," I answer with what even I know is a pathetic whine.

"I don't mean kissy-kissy likes you. I just mean, people have choices. She could tease you, she could ignore you, but instead she's coming over. She wouldn't do that if she hated you."

"She's just nice, that's all," I say. This whole line of questioning isn't territory I want to explore, so I add, "Anyway, it's no big deal," and "Not important." Then I throw in,

"Nothing to worry about," and finally, "Just thought I'd let you know."

So, after practice, when we come in the back door, I'm hoping Grandpa has gone out for a walk or taken up bowling or bird-watching. But no, he's sitting in the kitchen with his back to us. His laptop is on the table in front of him.

"Hey, Grandpa," I say.

"Be right with you, Superhero."

I try not to blush at the nickname and say quickly, "Uh, Grandpa? This is Heather."

Heather looks especially tall in our kitchen, and I think she feels it, too, because she's ducking her head just a little. When Grandpa turns around, she gives a shy little wave.

"Heather," he says, with a charm that surprises me. "What a wonderful name."

Heather shrugs. "Not everybody thinks so."

"Why not?" asks Grandpa. "A beautiful name for a beautiful girl."

I can't believe he says something so embarrassing, but Heather actually smiles. Maybe I've underestimated Grandpa. Or maybe you just get away with stuff like that when you're seventy-nine.

"It's just that 'Heather' sounds all breathy and wispy. People think of that song 'The Heather on the Hill,' and they think it's some dainty little flower that grows on a hillside.

Then they look at me and I'm . . ." She holds out her arms and sticks out one leg, to demonstrate just how un-wispy and un-dainty she is.

"Well," says Grandpa, and he moves his mouth the way he does sometimes, like he's tasting the words before he says them, "besides having a pretty purple flower, heather is a tough plant. It grows where practically everything else gives up, and comes back stronger every year."

"Yes!" cries Heather. She pulls out a chair and sits down next to Grandpa. "Exactly! It grows in Scotland, on the moors. And in Alaska. It's not delicate at all!"

"So, it's a perfect name, then," says Grandpa. "Joseph tells me you're a good runner. Right, Joseph?"

Heather looks at me like she's forgotten I'm here. She doesn't seem unpleasantly surprised, just surprised.

"I guess," she says. "I like running. I also want to throw shot put in winter and discus in spring."

"Heather told me about this girl," I break in. "She won a gold medal in discus."

"Stephanie Brown Trafton," says Heather. "Beijing Olympics—"

"Two thousand and eight," I finish, because I remember that's what Heather told me.

"You don't say," says Grandpa. "Is discus the flat one or the round one?"

"The flat one. It's like a heavy Frisbee. Shot put is like throwing a cannonball."

"Maybe you can get Joseph to try that." They both look at me and start laughing. Not at me, but . . . well, at me.

"No," says Heather, now perfectly serious. "Joseph is going to run distance. Indoor track in winter, outdoor in spring."

I am?

While I'm processing that little detail, Heather points to Grandpa's laptop. "What are you doing?" she asks him. She scooches her chair over, like they're old friends.

"I was just updating my Vintage Cupid profile," says Grandpa.

That gets my attention. "Your what?" I ask.

"Vintage Cupid."

"Is it like a dating site?" I say.

"It's exactly a dating site." I must look shocked. "What, you think I should just be playing bingo? Sitting around with the other old men *kvetching* and *grepsing*?"

Heather looks at me for an explanation and I look at Grandpa.

"After you eat, you sit around, *kvetching*." He waves his hand in circles, trying to find the right word. "Grousing. Complaining. And *grepsing*." He demonstrates with a long, exaggerated burp.

I now want to hide under the table or maybe in the broom closet, but Heather lets out a big laugh.

Then she points to the screen and asks, "Have you found anybody nice?"

Grandpa shrugs. Not the up-and-right-back-down kind of shrug, the kind where his shoulders stay up there. "I'm sure they're all nice ladies," he says. "But Sophie and I were married for fifty-three years." Now his shoulders drop and he looks at Heather. "You know the phrase 'my better half'? Well, Sophie was at least three quarters. Maybe seven eighths. Sometimes I wonder if there's any of me left at all."

Heather reaches over and pats Grandpa on the arm. "I think there's plenty of you left," she says. "More than most people I know."

Grandpa puts his hand on Heather's, and for a second I'm afraid Heather is going to add her other hand to the pile, too, but thank goodness she doesn't.

"Here," says Grandpa, turning the laptop toward us. "I'm going to take a nap. Do your French, then look for yourself. Tell me what you think." He takes a few steps and turns back. "But no golf. No long walks on the beach. They all want long walks. On the beach, in the woods, in the rain. Who wants to walk when it's raining outside? I want to see a movie, go to an opera. Not run a marathon. I'll leave that to you two." He turns to go. "And skip the ones who say they're seventy-nine," he adds.

"But, Grandpa, you're seventy-nine," I say.

"Trust me. The ones who put seventy-nine, they're eighty-five if they're a day."

"But what if somebody really is seventy-nine?" asks Heather.

"I'll wait until she's eighty," says Grandpa.

When Grandpa's gone, we take out our worksheets and start on French. Heather tries to explain the different ways of saying "to be." The first one is *être*, but saying it makes me choke. Then we go over the rest, including three different ways to say "are," and two "you"s.

After about half an hour, my head is spinning with "*je suis*" and "*tu es*" and "*nous sommes*," so it seems like the right time to take a look at Grandpa's computer. There are lots of pictures of smiling ladies. The ages they put down range from sixty to eighty-five, but nobody looks that old. I wonder if maybe the pictures are from a long time ago.

I point to a chubby lady holding a platter of what look like rugelach—a kind of pastry my grandma used to make. "She looks nice."

"Nope, look. Seventy-nine," says Heather. "How about her?" She clicks on a skinny woman with bright red hair.

"No," I say. "Golf."

We scroll through a few more listings. Grandpa's right. There are lots of old ladies who want to walk on the beach. And who love the rain. And lots of seventy-nine-year-olds.

Finally, we get to one picture of a white-haired lady sitting in a big chair reading a book. It's *David Copperfield*, by Charles Dickens. She looks familiar. I lean in closer and suddenly I realize why.

"Isn't that . . ." starts Heather.

"Mrs. Fishbein," I say.

"Mrs. Fishbein, the school librarian?"

I nod.

"Good books, movies, and music," Heather reads out loud. "Hot chocolate by a fire. Romantic moonlit nights . . ."

I slam the laptop shut before she can read any more. "Ew."

"But she's nice, isn't she?" Heather asks.

"Yeah, but . . ."

"Just because she's a teacher doesn't mean she doesn't get lonely," says Heather.

I think about those times I've seen Mrs. Fishbein leaving late, taking the bus home. "But Mrs. Fishbein hates computers," I say. "What's she doing on Vintage Cupid?"

"Maybe she hates being alone more than she hates computers."

Heather may be right, but I'm not at all ready for the idea of her and Grandpa and a moonlit night.

"Anyway," I say, "I don't think my grandpa would like her. She's really old-fashioned. She doesn't like anything new."

I hear the toilet flush and Grandpa rustling around. This must have been one of his quick naps. He comes into the kitchen and shakes a finger at the notepad sitting in front of me on the kitchen table, like it's done something wrong. "Joseph, write down, 'bar of soap.' Bar of soap. Some smartypants decided to bottle up the slime from a soap dish and everybody thinks it's wonderful, just because it's something new. I want a regular old bar of soap."

"Yeah, you're right. She's too old-fashioned. They'd just hate each other," Heather says, drumming her fingers on the laptop and looking at me like I'm the dumbest person in the world.

I write it down, making the letters of *BAR* extra large and underlining it. Grandpa looks over my shoulder to see that I've gotten it right.

"Well, I will retire to the den. It was a pleasure meeting you, Heather," Grandpa says, giving a little bow. "I hope I see you again soon."

"Maybe at the league meet. Are you coming?" Grandpa looks at me and then Heather says, "Joseph, you didn't invite your grandfather to the meet?"

"I meant to." Heather looks at me like I'm somebody's annoying little brother. "You should come, Grandpa. I'd like you to," I say.

"Then, I'll be there," says Grandpa.

Heather waves to Grandpa as he heads into the den. We hear some opera start up. I think it's in Italian. It doesn't sound any easier than French.

Heather quizzes me a few more times on those "to be" words. Then she looks at her watch. It's time for her to go home. She gathers up her stuff, but before she leaves, she stands in the doorway, glancing around the kitchen. "I like your grandpa. You're lucky," she says, and I think she's talking about more than Grandpa. "See you tomorrow."

I walk with her to the sidewalk and then watch her take long, leggy strides down the block. When she turns the corner, I go back inside and into the den, where Grandpa is settled in the recliner. I take my usual place on the chair arm.

"You know, I miss Grandma, too," I say. When I say it, I realize how much I really do miss her—her hugs, and her plum cake, and the way she decorated my birthday cards with little hearts and flowers. I even miss her off-key singing. I feel my eyes start to tear up.

"She was a grand lady," says Grandpa. "We met in third grade, you know."

"Really?" I didn't know that. Something else I never asked about.

"We were in Mrs. Offerman's class, and your grandma was sitting next to me. Someone the year before had ripped a page out of my math book. So, when Mrs. Offerman asked me the answer to question eight, I said I didn't have a question eight. She didn't believe me."

"She didn't believe you?"

"Nope." Grandpa leans closer and whispers, like even now he's afraid somebody will overhear and tell on him. "Mrs. Offerman was a nasty old coot. But your grandma sat up straight and she said, 'Freddie's book is missing that page.' Well, Mrs. Offerman didn't like that. Especially since Sophie forgot to raise her hand. She gave us both a look, but your grandma just said it again. 'Freddie doesn't have that page.' And Mrs. Offerman sent her out of the room. Out to the hallway! I'd been there a million times, but her, never. And she did it for me!"

For a minute, Grandpa almost looks like he's eight years old again, like he's still in love with that little girl who became my grandma.

"So you knew even then?" I ask.

"I didn't know that we'd be married. I had to hope and sweat and worry first. We all have to do that. It's part of being young. It goes with having a future. Now . . ." He waves his hand in the direction of the kitchen and the laptop. "All that computer nonsense. It's pretending, really. I'm not going to find another Sophie."

I don't know what to say. As creepy as Vintage Cupid is, at

least it's something. I don't want Grandpa to be sad and I don't want him to give up.

"Hey, Grandpa," I say, "do you remember that time when you took me to basketball practice?"

"With Mr. Cowboy Boots in charge?" he says.

"Yeah. And remember how you told me not to quit?" Grandpa nods. "Well, you shouldn't quit, either. I bet you can find somebody—not like Grandma—but, someone." He still doesn't look convinced, so I take a breath and put on a sterner voice and say, "And I don't think Grandma would want you to be sitting around *kvetching* and *grepsing*. Do you?"

Finally, Grandpa smiles. He sort of half pats, half grabs and shakes my shoulder. "Joseph, you're right. No, she wouldn't."

It crosses my mind to mention Mrs. Fishbein. But really, what could she talk about with Grandpa? School? Books? The Dewey Decimal system?

Grandpa stands and sends the chair rocking. I nearly fall off the recliner's arm. "I'm going to take a walk," he says. "Maybe I'll go down to the store and get myself a bar of soap. And then, who knows? Maybe I'll give Mr. Cupid another try."

I sit in the recliner for a minute after he's gone. Then I go to my room. I get on the floor and do some push-ups, and then some sit-ups. It still hurts, but I can do ten more than when I started. I do some more push-ups and some leg raises. Those really hurt. Enough for today.

I go to the mirror and pull up my shirt. I look closely. At first it doesn't look any different, but then I think I see something. I might be wrong, I probably am, but when I flex my stomach muscles, I think I see something.

Right there. Yup.

An ab.

CHAPTER 23

THE BUS THAT PULLS UP TO TAKE US TO OUR meet at Brockton Middle School is filled with football gear. The football team has a game tomorrow and they've preloaded the bus, which means, for one thing, it smells horrible, and for another, we can't spread out like we usually do. Heather doesn't seem to mind. She looks happy to be back on a bus, going to a track meet, even if it does smell like the inside of a football cleat. I sit next to Mark, and Sanjit sits with Wes. Across the aisle, Sammy has somehow gotten up the nerve to sit with Victoria and Heather sits down next to Coach T.

It's a bouncy ride; when we get close, the bus turns the corner and I see Brockton Middle School up ahead. I'm not sure if it's the turn and then the speed bump or the speed bump and then the turn, but the combination sends the bus rocking like a safari Jeep in one of those off-road commercials. Luckily my seatbelt keeps me from being catapulted like a cannonball, but not from whacking my head against the window. Twice. Brianne squeals when her water bottle flies out of her hand. Victoria gives a disgusted "Ew" and

shoves Sammy, who has been happily thrown sideways into her shoulder.

As we pull up in front of the school, I peer out the bottom half of the bus window. The top half is covered with some kind of grime I'd rather not think about. Brockton Middle School is nothing like Lakeview. Lakeview has three low buildings placed around a central courtyard, with covered breezeways, so you can walk from building to building without getting wet. Brockton is a huge stone building that looks like some kind of English castle. The front doors are dark and wooden. They must be about a foot thick, with heavy iron latches. It makes me wonder if all the kids who go in there come out at the end of the day.

The bus makes that squeaky, exhausted *ppppphhhtt* sound that means we're here. Victoria pushes her way past Sammy, but Coach T says, "Wait here, guys."

Coach tries all three front doors. They're all locked. She looks up at the bus driver, who shrugs, but then a lanky kid comes around the corner and says something, pointing around the far side of the building.

"Okay, we're meeting around back," she says, stepping back onto the bus. "Make sure you take your gear. Let's go."

We file off and start walking around the building. I look up. There are these faces carved into the corners, looking down at me. Some look studious, some look stern, but the worst are the ones that are smiling, with open, toothless, creepy-looking mouths.

"Gargoyles," says Heather.

"Huh?" I say, and she points up.

"Those faces. That's what they're called."

Gargoyles are now officially on my list of things I'm afraid of. I'll put them somewhere between party clowns and Mr. Peanut. I try not to look up for the rest of the walk, but even without seeing them, I know those gargoyles are watching me with their stone faces and frozen eyes.

Finally, we get to the back lawn. The school building seems to cast its gloomy shadow over the school grounds. The air feels cold and damp, and the sky is like a big gray roll of cotton. It all gives me the shivers.

We walk past the Brockton team lined up on the grass in their dark green singlets and shorts, stretching like they're made out of rubber bands instead of flesh and bone. They don't seem to feel the cold at all. They all have matching haircuts, short on the sides and brushed up in the middle, and they're all between five foot five and five foot nine. Nobody's fat and there's not a pair of glasses in sight.

"Their high school team won five state championships in the past ten years," says Heather. Looking at this bunch, I'd say they're prepping for at least five more.

Brockton's coach blows a whistle and all the Brockton kids

stop stretching. They stand up so straight, I think they might salute. Their coach is stuffed into a green Brockton Bears sweatshirt and has one of those walrus mustaches that covers his mouth and makes you wonder how he eats at all. Judging from the size of his stomach, he finds a way.

"All right, runners!" he calls out. His voice is higher than you'd expect. He sounds a little like my uncle Monty from Boston. "They tell me there might be a stawm blowin' in . . ."

"A what?" whispers Mark.

"A storm," says Heather.

". . . so we're gonna skip the walk-through and get right to the race. The course is clearly marked, across the field, into the woods, and back here. If you're not sure where to go, just follow my runners. They'll most likely be in front of you anyway." He chuckles at his own humor. "And with the stawm comin', we're going to run everybody at once: boys and girls together."

"Seriously?" says Brianne.

"Sounds good to me," says Sammy. He slides over next to Victoria.

"Now, I expect everyone to be courteous. Although I doubt ladies will be first."

"Wanna bet?" mutters Heather.

The Brockton coach looks up at the sky. The clouds are getting thicker, and the air is heavy and still. "Okay, so let's get going!"

All of the Brockton runners start to line up even before the ref calls out, "Everybody, line up! Boys and girls!" The ref gives a worried glance up at the sky and scratches his bald head. He's standing in front of a tree that looks a lot like him. Its leaves are mostly orange, but the top has already wilted and blown away.

The girl next to me is retying her sneakers, then she re-rubber-bands her ponytail. A few places away, Heather is staring straight ahead, picking up one foot, then the other, like a horse at the starting gate.

"And remember," the ref shouts, "if you hear even a rumble of thunder, come straight back here. Safety first!"

Sanjit is next to me, shaking out his arms to loosen up, and Erica is beside him, looking tiny and very nervous. Sanjit pats her on the shoulder and she smiles up at him. She definitely likes Sanjit. I see the ref raise the starting gun. I fumble around with my earplugs and manage to get them in just in time.

Blam!

The Brockton boys take off, and Heather is right up front with them. Wes and Sammy try to stay close, but the rest of us spread out as we go across the field. I'm pretty far back, but there are a few other slow and unfocused kids nearby, and some girls who are barely running. They're side by side and I can hear them talking about boy bands.

I follow the arrows chalked on the field and try not to worry about my pace or what Charlie Kastner would say if he knew that most of the girls are ahead of me. I listen for thunder, but so far there's just the sound of feet on dirt and the coaches' shout-outs to their runners.

I watch as the woods swallow kids up, one by one, and I can feel the stares of those gargoyles behind me. When I finally reach the woods myself, I'm already breathing hard. Under all the trees, it's like someone has pulled down a shade. I can hear the wind start to whistle in the bare branches above me. I wish Fox Ridge was running in this meet. It would be nice to have Heber here for company.

I keep putting one foot ahead of the other and I can hear myself breathing. I'm starting to sweat. There's an actual brook running through the course, and little wooden bridges that cross over and back. The sound my feet make when I cross the bridges is comforting, sort of a hollow *thump, thump*. The water is splashing along, making little bubbling sounds. I take a walk break and I'm almost enjoying myself, until I come around a curve where the branches thin out into spindly fingers and I can see the school building and its gargoyles. What kind of people build a place for kids with scary faces on it, anyway? When I come to the next bridge, I race across. I'm sure there's a troll lurking underneath, waiting to pounce.

The course starts to go uphill, and I'm trying not to trip,

to just keep going and not make too much of a fool of myself. I've actually caught up to some of the other runners. There are maybe five of us within a few yards of each other. I make a turn, and ahead of me I see a couple of kids moving to the right side of the trail. They're going around something that's in the way. As I get closer I see that it's not a something, it's a someone.

It's Heather.

She's off to the side of the path, leaning on a tree. At first it looks like she's just taking a breather, but Heather would never take a breather. Not in a million years. And she should be way up ahead by now.

My heart is pumping and I'm trying to catch my breath. "What happened?" I ask, stopping next to her.

"You're in a race, Friedman," she snaps. "What are you stopping for?" Now I see that her left knee is bleeding. She's standing on her right leg, holding the hurt one up. She has a scratch on her cheek and some more on her arms.

"I'm stopping," I say, taking a breath, "because . . . what happened?"

"A Brockton guy threw an elbow. He wanted to pass, and I didn't let him."

"You were ahead of the Brockton boys?" I know that's not the point, but still.

She keeps talking, but it's like I'm eavesdropping on

a conversation she's having with herself. "I wasn't ready for it. It was stupid. I should've just pushed him back." She demonstrates with a sharp jab of her elbow. "I should've pushed him into the stupid bushes!"

The girls who were behind me walk by. When they hear Heather they speed up to a nervous trot and scurry past.

Heather picks up a stick and hurls it across the path. I'm a little afraid I'll be next.

"Where's the rest of the team?" I ask. "Didn't they see you?"

She points to a spot on the ground behind her, off the trail. "I was over there. They didn't see me."

"You should've called them. They could've helped . . ."

"They were in a race," she snaps. "And so are you. Stop looking at me and go." I don't move. "Go!"

I know she's mad and I'm almost afraid to stay, but I don't feel like I can go. She looks angry, but like she wants to cry, too. And there's that friend thing. If I'm her friend, I should help.

"It doesn't make a difference," I say. "I'm last, anyway."

"And you're okay with that?" says Heather. "You're happy to be last?"

"I'm not happy to be," I say. "I just am."

I can hear cheering in the distance. Probably the Brockton boys are finishing, or maybe they came in a long time ago and it's the first girl. I've sort of lost track of who's where.

"You just are?" says Heather. "What's wrong with you, anyway, Friedman? You don't fight. You let other kids trample you. You duck when the ball is coming. You don't even mind being last."

I know she's saying all this because she's upset, but my breath catches in my chest for a second, anyway, like it does when Charlie Kastner laughs at me for dropping a ball. Like it did when Mary Liz glared at me in third grade.

"I mind," I say.

"Then do something!"

"Like what?" I half yell. "What exactly am I supposed to do? Magically make myself a good athlete? Become the coolest kid in the grade? Wake up a genius?"

I feel like walking away. Or running. Like Heather said, I'm in a race. I should just leave her here, if that's what she wants. I even take a step to go.

"You can fight back," says Heather. "Stop ducking and fight back."

That's when we hear the thunder. Perfect. I'm not going to leave her here, with a thunderstorm on the way. Besides, I know deep down that I wasn't going to leave her anyway. I put out my hand. She looks like she'd rather punch me than admit she needs help, but when she tries to take a step on her own, she grimaces.

"Come on," I say. I keep my hand out until finally she takes it and puts her weight on her right foot. She leans on me like I've seen people do when they've been hurt in a football game or a war. It's a lot harder than it looks, and I almost go down. But once I get my balance and she gets hers, we limp along and do okay.

We make our way through the woods into the open field, where we can see the finish line. The thunder is rumbling, but it sounds pretty far away. We're probably not going to get hit by lightning. Still, nothing would surprise me.

Coach T is running toward us, and she meets us before we get to the finish line. "What happened?" she says, a little out of breath. "I was coming to find you!" She eases Heather from my shoulder onto hers.

"A guy elbowed me," says Heather.

"Who?" asks Coach T.

There's another low rumble of thunder. "Some Brockton kid."

"Can you point him out?"

"I don't know," she says. "They all have that same stupid haircut." Coach T looks over her shoulder. The visiting teams are hurrying to the buses. The Brockton kids are heading into the school. "Here," she says. She shoulders Heather back over to me like a bag of groceries, and goes after them.

It surprises me, how fast she runs. She catches up to the Brockton coach and he points to the sky, but she grabs his arm and says something else. Then he calls the boys over. We can see from here how they all shake their heads, how one of them points to the ground and shrugs, and how the coach holds his hands in a sign of helplessness, says something to Coach T, and motions to the boys to go inside.

There's a louder boom of thunder, and Coach T calls for us all to hurry to the bus. Mark takes Heather's other side and we help her along. As the Brockton team heads back inside, one kid looks over his shoulder with a smirky smile and I know it's him. I just know he's the one who pushed her.

We dash for the bus, with Heather between us. Just as the bus doors whoosh shut, the rain starts. A few seconds later, it's pouring down in sheets.

"What did they say?" I ask Coach T as we take seats. She's pulling an instant ice pack out of the medical bag in a way that reminds me of my mother when she's upset and banging around in the kitchen.

"They all denied it. One said a girl tripped, but it had nothing to do with them."

"And the coach believed them?" Wes asks.

"Of course," she snaps. "They're Brockton. They're little angels."

There isn't a peep from anybody. I exchange a wide-eyed glance with Sanjit, but we all keep quiet. I guess I'm not the only one who's had a parent in this kind of mood.

The bus lurches into motion, and as we click our seatbelts, Heather says, "I should've just caught up to that kid and punched him out."

"And you've had good luck with that in the past," says Coach T in a Mrs. T warning tone of voice.

I almost smile.

"I'll call their coach again tomorrow," says Coach T. "I'm not going to let that little—" She must see ten middle school mouths drop open all at once, and she stops herself just in time. "I'll make sure he doesn't let it happen again."

I've never seen this side of Coach T, or Mrs. T for that matter. I kind of like it.

She adjusts the ice pack on Heather's ankle a little roughly. "Ice it now, and more when you get home. Your dad can take you to see the doctor. We have plenty of time until the league meet. Let's hope it's just a sprain."

The bus bounces along, rain pounding the roof, splashing the windows as we dip into potholes. I sit across the aisle from Heather. She has the whole seat, with her leg stretched out and the ice pack on her ankle.

"You heard Coach," I say. "You'll rest it before the league meet. It's probably just a sprain."

She still looks pretty grumpy.

"I hope you don't expect me to stop for you," she says. "If I'm in a race, and you're down, I wouldn't stop."

"Yes, you would," I say.

"Would not."

"Would too."

That's all we say for the rest of the ride, but I know I'm right. She would do the same for me. She already has.

CHAPTER 24

IT'S NOT THAT I'VE FORGOTTEN WHAT HEATHER said on the trail, or that I've decided she was right. Although I have to admit, some of it was true: I don't fight. I let other kids trample me. I duck when the ball is coming and I don't really mind being last. Still, it's not like I don't try at all. In fact, I've been trying pretty hard. But when she comes into school with her sprained ankle wrapped like a mummy, it doesn't seem like the right time to talk about it. Even if I wanted to.

There are ten days before the league meet, and Heather has to rest her ankle for at least a week. The doctor says there's a fifty-fifty chance that she'll be one-hundred-percent ready to run. That makes no sense to me. I guess all he's really saying is, *Let's hope for the best.*

Meanwhile, Coach T has appointed Heather as her assistant coach, so she can still be involved with the team and not get too down. Coach T also tells us that we better get ready for some serious training. She says we're even going to have a practice on Wednesday.

When my parents agree to let me skip Hebrew school, I'm thrilled. But that's before I hear Coach T's goal for the day: We'll be running up White Oak Lane, not just once, but three times in a row.

I find myself wishing I were at Beth Shalom, reciting Torah blessings.

"You're going to make this hill your friend," says Coach T. "When everybody else is struggling, you'll be jogging up White Oak, whistling your favorite song."

Sure.

As our new assistant coach, Heather stands at the top of White Oak and yells at us.

"Come on, Sammy, even strides, no kindergarten steps! Victoria, no drama queens! Wes, you're going to let Erica pass you?!" And the one that really gets me: "Friedman, no kvetching!" She wouldn't even know that word if it weren't for me.

I can't wait until she can run again.

We repeat that workout on Thursday, and on Friday, Coach T tells us we're going to give White Oak Lane a rest. She tells us she has another workout she wants us to try.

It's called a fartlek.

"A what?" says Sammy. His mouth is wide open and his eyebrows are crinkled up. It's almost too good to believe, a word like that. "It's called a what?"

"A fartlek," says Coach T. "It's a series of exercises that

combines stamina, speed, and agility . . ." She looks up and sighs. "Okay, go ahead. You've got two minutes."

She times us while Wes and Sammy roll on the grass laughing their heads off, and we all take turns saying it out loud and cracking up. Every time we settle down, someone says, "Fartlek," and we all start up again. Mark says it in an especially funny way, making it buzz in his throat. At first, Erica and Teresa are pretending to be grossed out, and Heather is looking at us like we're ridiculous, but then they start laughing, too, and even Erica takes a turn saying it.

Coach T actually gives us more than our two minutes, and when we finally settle down to a smattering of giggles and snorts, she explains what a fartlek is. Suddenly it doesn't sound so funny. It sounds more like a form of torture, invented in Sweden.

First you warm up. Then you run for a while, then you walk fast, then you go back to running, and then when the coach says so you have to sprint as fast as you can. Then you run some more and take some quick little steps, the kind you'd have to use if somebody's trying to pass you. Then you run as fast as you can again. Then you're supposed to repeat all of that until you feel like a bowl of Jell-O, or herring, or whatever jiggly food they have in Sweden.

So on Friday and Monday, we do our fartleks. I go home

with sore calf muscles and thigh muscles and everything muscles and eat half the refrigerator before dinner.

But on Tuesday, we learn another new word. A good word: *tapering*. That means doing less. Much less. Until the meet, we'll be tapering, just loosening up with "shake-out" runs, which means short and easy. We're saving up our energy for the league meet on Friday. *Tapering* is now my favorite word.

After practice, I head back into school. There's something I've been wanting to do.

I've had my copy of *Get in Shape, Boys!* in my backpack for about four days now, and I'm determined not to lug it home and back even one more time. I still don't look like Pete Power, and I don't think I'm ever going to. But Pete Power has probably never even heard of a fartlek, so I might have something over him.

I head to the library and open the door. I don't see Mrs. Fishbein. I wander to the back and peer into her office. No one.

I hear the library door open and Mrs. Fishbein's footsteps coming toward her office. I step out where she can see me and say, "Hi, Mrs. Fishbein," so I don't scare her.

I scare her anyway.

"Oh, Joseph," she says, her hand over her heart. "I wasn't expecting anyone."

The last thing I want to do is give Mrs. Fishbein a heart attack. I hold up the book and say, "I wanted to return this. Should I leave it up front?"

"No, sweetheart, just leave it in there on my desk. That radar gun is on the fritz again." She waves at the checkout machine, like she wishes it would just go away. "Did you enjoy it? The book?"

I don't know if *enjoy* is the word, but I say, "Yes. I mean, it was kind of helpful. I'm running cross country now."

"Well, that's wonderful," she says. "You've become a real athlete."

"I wouldn't say that," I say, but I like the sound of it anyway.

"Would you like a Cup O' Noodles?" she asks, stepping into her office.

I definitely would not like a Cup O' Noodles, not only because of those slimy, wormy noodles, but also because that would mean staying to talk, and I can't think of anything now when I look at Mrs. Fishbein except for her Vintage Cupid page.

"Thanks, but I really have to get home," I say. I don't wear a watch, but I look at my wrist to make it seem more pressing. "Lots of homework," I add.

But when I put *Get in Shape, Boys!* on her desk, I knock over a framed picture. When I scramble to catch it, I end up knocking down two more, and then they all start falling like dominoes, with me chasing after them.

"I'm really sorry," I say, trying to get the pictures to stay up on their flimsy little stands. But as soon as I get one to stay, another falls.

"Don't worry, Joseph," she says. "Really. They're old frames. They're old pictures."

I look down at the one that's in my hand. It's Mrs. Fishbein with a man in a hat on an old boat. She takes it gently from me.

"Inishbofin," she says, like she's casting a magic spell.

"What?"

"We went to an island called Inishbofin. My husband and I. That was our last trip together, in Ireland, on our way to this silly little island called Inishbofin. He passed away five years ago." She looks at me and asks, "Can you stay? Just for a minute?"

It would be pretty mean to leave after the mess I made and just as she's telling me about her husband who died, so I sit down on a chair—luckily, a wooden one, not the slippery gray kind.

She points at the picture. "Look how rusty that ferry is. We thought it would sink right in the middle of the ride. But it got us there. We rented bikes and the paths took us right through the sheep pastures, to the very edge of the cliffs. The sheep were everywhere, long-haired sheep, all soggy from the rain. You wanted to squeeze them out, like a kitchen mop in a bucket. And people had their laundry hanging on clotheslines. Reds and oranges and bright greens flapping against the blue of the sea."

Maybe Mrs. Fishbein should have been a poet instead of a librarian.

"It sounds nice," I say.

"Oh, it was so beautiful." She looks off into space, like she's imagining it all again. So I'm surprised when she says, "And then I hit a rock and my bicycle tire blew out."

"Oh, no," I say.

"But that's the thing! Sometimes the best things happen when things go wrong. We missed our ferry back and stayed overnight in a little bed-and-breakfast. We had potato-leek soup for dinner and Irish brown bread. It was perfect. If I hadn't run over that rock, we would never have seen that perfect sunset or the full moon that night . . ."

Romantic, moonlit nights.

"Do you like to travel, Joseph?"

"I . . . don't know," I answer, pulling my mind away from the moonlit cliffs of Inishbofin and back to the library. "I've been to Vermont and once we went to Florida, but I've never been anywhere like Inishbofin. I'd like to."

"Oh, would you?" says Mrs. Fishbein. "I'm too old to go

back now." She sighs. "I'm a pretty tough old goose, but without Artie it's hard."

"My grandpa says stuff like that, too. How he'll never find someone else like . . ." I cut myself off and start again. "You're not too old at all." I look at my wrist again and say, "I've really got to go."

"Of course," she says. "Of course, don't let me keep you."

I look at Mrs. Fishbein, still holding the picture, still thinking about Inishbofin. I know she'll be going home by herself, maybe to look at Vintage Cupid on the computer she hates.

I think about Grandpa and how much he misses my grandma. That must be how Mrs. Fishbein feels. And Eddie, back at Sunshine Senior Living. I realize how unfair it is for all of them to be alone.

And before I even think it through, I say, "Mrs. Fishbein? Do you want to come to my cross country meet on Friday?"

"Your . . ."

"Cross country meet. It's the last race of the season. It's here, at Lakeview. It starts near the track. Lots of teams are coming. It's the league meet."

"Do you think you might win?"

"Me? No!" She looks surprised. I guess it seems weird to invite someone to a race where you don't have any chance of winning. I try to explain. "I'm not a very good runner. But there's something called a PR, a personal record. It's when you try to do better than the last time. I'll be trying for a personal record."

"Well, that's a sport I'd love to watch," she says. "Will your parents be there?"

"I think so," I say. "And my grandpa," I throw in.

"How lovely. I'll do my best to be there."

I smile and nod and give Mrs. Fishbein a thumbs-up. Then I leave the library without giving a hint that I know anything about Vintage Cupid, or hot chocolate by a fire, or being lonely.

CHAPTER 25

IT'S ALREADY THURSDAY. THE LEAGUE MEET IS tomorrow, and I'm waiting for Heather outside our French class. She went to see the doctor this morning—at least, I think she did. She's been running with us at practices, just a little at a time, but the doctor has to give her an all-clear so she can race tomorrow. I keep imagining her coming down the hall, telling me she's gotten the all-clear, then warning me that even though she's not the assistant coach anymore I shouldn't expect any mercy.

This is not a position I usually place myself in. Standing still in school hallways has always invited trouble. Historically, I've gotten bumped and banged, been the target of half-eaten cupcakes, seen kids elbowing their friends, whispering some story about what a dork I was in sixth grade. Or kindergarten. Or yesterday. I'm standing close to the door into French, just in case Charlie and Zachary come along and I need a safety zone. They've pretty much kept their distance since Charlie's nose's encounter with Heather's fist, but you never know when they'll decide it's time to get back in the let's-get-Friedman game.

But so far, so good. In fact, today I get a nod, an actual nod, from Danielle Symington, and then Billy Hayward says, "Hey, man." I'm not sure how to respond, so I raise my hand in greeting, and it seems to go over pretty well.

I'm basking in my newfound popularity when the halls start to empty and I realize the bell will ring soon. I wonder if the doctor was late. I wonder if Heather got bad news. Then wonder turns to worry, and I start to count all the reasons why she might be late, all the reasons she might not be able to run. Maybe her ankle isn't healed. Maybe she got the okay, but then tripped coming down the stairs from the doctor's office and broke her arm. Maybe she got locked in the bathroom or has a stomach virus. All the maybes go flashing through my mind, but then, just as I'm about to give up and go in to French, I see Heather coming down the hall.

I'm having trouble standing still. I'm bouncing on my toes, and finally I run up to her and barely resist the urge to tug at her sleeve like a terrier puppy.

"So?" I say. "What did the doctor say? Are you healed? Can you run?"

"I guess," says Heather, which is way below a yes.

"What do you mean? Can you race or not?"

Heather tries to pass me and go in the door to French. "We have a quiz," she says, but I get in front of her and say, "Tell me what happened with the doctor. What did he say?"

"She's a she, and she said I could run, okay?"

I can't figure out why she's not happy. "So that's great, right?"

"She said I should 'go easy.'"

"But that's nothing," I say, relieved. "You could hop on one leg and probably still beat everybody."

"Stephanie Brown Trafton would never agree to 'go easy.'" Then she stops and looks down and says, "My mom called last night. She wants us to move. To Hawaii."

Just then the bell slams my eardrums. My heart starts to race, not just because we're standing right under the speaker, but because I can't believe what Heather just said.

I look at the open door, but I can't go into French now. I can't. I need more time. I need to do something. Heather is carrying her drawing pad and a plastic box filled with colored pencils. I do the only thing I can think of. I reach out and grab the pencil box, pull the lid open, and throw the whole thing on the floor.

"*Mes étudiants*," Madame Labelle sings out, coming to the doorway. "*Entrez-vous, s'il vous plaît.*" Shockingly, I understand her. She's saying, "My students, come in please."

Then she sees the pencils. They're scattered all over the place. An orange one is spinning down the hallway and a few are rolling into that grubby space under the lockers. I put on my guiltiest face and say, "Oh, Madame. *Je suis* . . . um . . . *stupide. Je* . . ." I wave my arms around like a crazy person to show her how I accidentally knocked into Heather and spilled the pencils. *"Et je . . ."* I point to Heather and then to me and pantomime that I'm going to help Heather pick them all up. Then I put my palms together like I'm pleading. *"Deux minutes, s'il vous plaît?"*

Maybe it's the shock of hearing even part of a French sentence coming out of my mouth, or maybe she's impressed by my acting ability, but Madame looks at us, nods, and says, *"Eh bien. Mais vite! Vite!"* which I think must mean just hurry it up already.

As soon as she closes the door, Heather turns to me. "What was that?"

"It was all I could think of," I say.

"All you could think of to what?"

"To . . . I don't know. To find out what happened."

Heather looks at the pencils scattered all over the place. She gathers up about six and then leans on the wall, holding the pencils like a bunch of flowers. She lets herself slide down along the wall and sits on the floor. I pick up some more pencils and stand next to her. I try sliding down the wall the same way, but it doesn't go smoothly. I lose control and land way too hard.

"Ow. So what happened?" I ask. "Your mom. What did she say?"

"First she talked about that hibiscus again."

"The one that changes color?"

Heather nods. "She keeps saying how much she loves it. How she loves everything in Hawaii and she can't bear to leave."

I don't say anything. I just wait for Heather to go on.

"She thinks we'd all be happy there. She wants us to come. My dad and me."

"To stay?"

She nods.

"But that's like a million miles away." I hear my voice rising to a fourth-grade squeak.

"My dad says she should just come home. He says she'll get tired of Hawaii and want to go somewhere else. They were arguing. I've never heard them argue like that."

She opens the box and puts her bunch of pencils back inside.

"Do you want to go?" I ask, even though I'm afraid to hear the answer.

She shrugs. "We'd all be together. And it sounds really beautiful. My mom says it's sunny practically every day there. You can surf all year and there are palm trees and coconuts."

I want to say that coconuts fall on your head and sunburn gives you cancer and sharks eat surfers for breakfast. I want to say, "What happens when she wants you to go to Thailand, or New Mexico, or that place with the plants that eat frogs?"

Most of all, I want to yell, "Don't go! I don't want you to! Don't go!"

The late bell screams and Heather gets up. She walks down the hall and picks up the orange pencil that's made it halfway to the science lab. I fish under the locker behind me and manage to find two more. It's disgusting under there, but I pluck them up with two fingers, trying to leave the dust balls and grit behind.

"The thing I don't understand," says Heather, "is you're supposed to be in love with people, not places."

I think about Mrs. Fishbein and Grandpa. How places seem empty without the people they love. Maybe it's not like that for Heather's mom. Or maybe she's realizing that it is.

"She's calling again tomorrow night," says Heather, "to give me time to think about it. But I don't know what to say."

I can't believe I have an answer to that, but I do. It seems like the only advice that seems right. "Just tell her the truth," I say. I just wish I knew what that will turn out to be.

We both head toward the classroom door, but before she opens it, Heather says, "Remember, *J'ai, tu as, nous avons, vous avez.*"

"What?" I say.

"The quiz. *J'ai, tu as, nous avons, vous avez.*"

"Oh. Oh, yeah. Got it."

I follow her in and Madame Labelle motions for us to

hurry and sit down. Everybody else has started the quiz. It's on the verb *avoir*, "to have." It's almost as hard as *être*, "to be."

I look at the first question: *"As-tu une amie?"* Do you have a friend?

I write down *"Oui, j'ai une amie."*

I hope it's the right answer.

CHAPTER 26

"I FEEL SICK," SAYS WES.

I doubt that anybody's stomach is feeling too great, since it's the afternoon of the league meet and it's a quarter to four. But I have to admit, Wes looks worse than the rest of us. Ten schools have come to Lakeview, and we're all here in our uniforms, in red and blue and orange and green and purple, with school names shouting from our chests. I made sure to wash my singlet myself last night. Unfortunately, Grandpa's new red T-shirt was in there already, so my Lakeview Leopards blue is now a pale lavender.

Wes moans and rubs his stomach.

"What did you have for lunch?" Sammy asks him.

"A cherry Pop-Tart."

"Frosted?" asks Mark.

"Duh," says Wes. "And some chips I found in my locker."

"Barbecue?"

"Dill pickle," says Wes.

"I think we have a winner," Sammy says.

There's a roped-off chute that leads to the finish line,

and it's all decorated with Lakeview blue flags that wave in the wind. It seems like there are a million people here, and cheers break out every few minutes for Panthers and Bears and Hornets. Most of the other schools have seventh- and eighth-grade teams, but since this is our first year, we only have seventh. And seventh grade goes first.

I'm trying to get into the festive mood, but I can't. Heather wasn't at practice yesterday. Coach gave her the afternoon off to rest her ankle, but it's not like Heather to stay away just because somebody said she could. She didn't answer my texts, and today she came in to both French and Science late and slipped out before I could even talk to her. I couldn't even tell her that I somehow got a B+ on the French quiz.

And now it's the league meet and she's not here.

All the visiting teams have walked the course—across the field, through the woods, up White Oak, behind the gym, then back. In the race we'll go back into the woods for a second time around. Victoria led the visiting girls and Sanjit led the boys.

Coach T is standing a few paces away, holding a clipboard and looking over a list of names.

I walk over to her. "Coach," I say.

She holds up a finger and spends about three more seconds staring at the papers. Then she turns to me, and even though she smiles, I see a little bit of worry on her face. Her eyes aren't crinkling the way they usually do.

"Heather's not here," I say.

"I know," she answers.

"I talked to her yesterday and her mom . . . she might . . ."

Coach T nods. "I know. She told me." She looks at her watch. "But she said she'd be here for the meet. I know it means a lot to her." She puts her hand on my arm and says, "There's so much going on in Heather's life right now."

"Coach!" calls Sammy. "Who's first? Boys or girls?"

Coach T lets Sammy's question just hang there. "Are you okay?" she asks me.

"I guess," I say, but I wish things were different.

"Heather will be all right. And you're going to run a great race. A PR. I know you will." She turns toward Sammy and the rest of the team. "Girls are first," she calls out. She gives my arm a squeeze, then lets go and waves us all in. It's time for our pep talk.

When we gather around, Sanjit says, "Hey, why isn't Heather here?"

Teresa looks over at Heather's usual stretching tree. "Coach T," she asks, "where's Heather?"

"Don't worry," says Coach T. "I'm sure she'll be here."

Coach T's husband brought their bulldogs, George and Ringo. They join our circle and sit on either side of Coach

T, like bodyguards. I sit on the ground next to Ringo. I rub the place where his neck slopes down to his shoulders. It's fat and sturdy and smooth all at once. He smiles up at me and it makes me feel a little better, but Coach T reaches around him and pats me on the shoulder, to make sure I'm listening to everything she has to say.

She tells us how proud she is of all of us. How much we've all improved. How this is our school's first time hosting the league's final middle school meet and we'll always know, for the rest of our lives, that we were part of it. Then she gives us some final words of advice.

"All of you, remember the work we've put in. All the times you've run up White Oak Lane. All the fartleks."

Even now, Sammy can't hold in a laugh.

"There are a lot of runners today. More than you're used to. I want you to stay in a pack and go out fast. We want good position when we funnel into the woods, but then slow down. Pace yourselves. You know the course. Save something for the second time around, then"—she throws up her hands—"give it your all."

She looks around the circle, focusing in on each one of us for a few seconds. Then she says, "I'm depending on you to help one another. Boys, support the girls. Girls, cheer the boys on. I'm going to be over at the finish. I'll try to get to the halfway point, but I know you can do it without me. Be a team. Run strong and try hard. That's all I can ask. It's all you can ask of yourselves." She looks around at us one more time. "You know the course better than anybody. You know the woods. You've run the hill. There are no surprises, other than how you're going to surprise yourselves." She claps her hands. "So let's go stretch, warm up. Have a great race!"

I look around. JFK is here, and Fox Ridge, New Kingsfield, Hampton, Cross River, Eagleton, even two private schools, Xavier Prep and St. Aloysius. Their names alone scare me.

And then there's Brockton. The boys' team is gathered in a huddle, right near the tree where I left my backpack. One kid is talking. When I get close, I hear words like "win" and "position" and then the word "wimps," and they all laugh.

I feel a tap on my shoulder. I jump about ten feet and turn. It's Heber. He's wearing a light green T-shirt under his singlet, which is sort of a maroonish purple. He looks like a gigantic pistachio nut.

"Hey," he says.

"Hey," I answer.

"Have you gotten any faster?" he asks. "Because I haven't."

"Maybe," I say. "Not a lot, but a little faster."

"Well, don't hang back with me, then. I only seem to get slower and slower."

"Well, maybe today's the day."

"Yeah. Maybe."

The ref blows his whistle. "Girls, line up!"

I see four girls in Lakeview blue standing together, and I feel a catch in my throat.

I hear the ref say, "Ready!" and I dig into my backpack, fumbling around to find my earplugs. I have one pair left.

"Set . . ." calls the ref. I put the earplugs in, press my hands to my head as hard as I can, and close my eyes.

Blam!

I hear muffled laughter. I open my eyes, look to my right, and see the Brockton boys. They're not watching the girls' race, they're watching me. One of them has his hands over his ears and his eyes squeezed closed, imitating me.

I try to ignore them and pull out my earplugs, placing them carefully in my backpack's side pocket, so I can find them again before my race.

"Hey," Heber says, "look at that girl." I stand up and it takes me a few seconds to refocus. When I do, I see a light blue jersey, coming fast from the far right. She has to cover twice the ground that the others do just to get to the center of the field. Her ankle is bandaged, but her hair is flying, her stride long and graceful. Soon she's crossed the whole field, and by the time they go into the woods she's near the front. She's not "going easy," but I never thought she would.

"Heather!" I call out as they slip into the trees. "Go, Heather!" I'm not sure if she hears me, but I scream as loud as I can.

Now everybody troops over to the midway point by the gym, where the girls will come out after they've run the woods. It'll be a few minutes, but everyone wants a good place to watch. "Come on," I say to Heber, and he bounces along next to me.

"Is that girl your girlfriend?" he asks.

"Not a girlfriend. A friend."

"Still," he says. "Do you think she could win?"

"She usually does," I answer.

"Boy, I want your life," says Heber, and I stop for a second and wonder how things have advanced to the point that anybody would say that.

Everybody's crowded by the corner of the gym. The runners will be out in the open for a few hundred yards and then head back to the woods for their second loop. We wait and wait, until finally we see them.

Heather is in the lead. The JFK girl is close, but she's no match for Heather. It doesn't look like Heather's ankle is giving her any trouble, or if it is, it doesn't show.

I yell as loud as I can, "Heather! Come on, Heather!" I hear Sammy and Wes shouting too, and then Mark and Sanjit. Even Heber joins in.

She picks up the pace, and as she goes into the woods for the second time, she leaves the JFK girl even farther behind. We wait for Victoria and Teresa, and then after a couple more minutes, Brianne and Erica come through.

We have a few minutes until they come around again. I scan the crowd for Grandpa, or my parents, or even Mrs. Fishbein. I don't see any of them.

But I see someone else: Heather's dad. He's standing on a hill, under a tall, leafless maple tree. I leave the others and run up to him. There isn't a lot of time. "Over here," I say, pulling him down toward the course. I don't give him a chance to say anything. I just want him to see Heather finish.

Instead of pushing into the crowd, where everyone's clustered to get a first look, I take him over to the finish chute. There's a rope to mark the course, and I put him next to it, where she'll be sure to see him. "She'll be coming through there," I tell him, and before he can say anything, before he can catch my eye and give me any news I don't want to hear, I hurry away. I can't bear to think that Heather's next race might be in Hawaii.

I run back to join the team and wait for the runners to come around the gym.

We don't have to wait long. I hear a cheer start to my left. They're the first ones who can see the leader. As she turns the corner, the rest of us can see the girl who's out in front.

It's Heather.

We yell her name and Sammy is jumping up and down and Sanjit is calling out, "Go! Strong to the finish!" She's around the corner on her way across the field toward the finish chute.

The other girls haven't even come around the corner. We all know that Heather has it won.

Except, instead of accelerating to the finish, she slows down. She takes a few steps and stops, right in the middle of the course. She's looking at her dad, who is doing the strangest thing. He's putting one fist over the other and switching them, left over right, right over left.

Maybe it's another one of those meaningless signals they use to trick their opponents. But it can't be, because she's the only one who's watching. It isn't meant to fool anybody. It's only meant for Heather.

The JFK girl can't be that far behind. Heather has to start running again. But she doesn't. She doesn't run at all. She walks over to her dad and throws her arms around him. He wraps her in a hug, the rope and the little blue flags between them. He says something and points to the finish, but she shakes her head. I try to imagine what's going on, but I can't. It looks like Heather is crying, but maybe it's happy crying or maybe it's sad crying. I just don't know.

"What's she doing?" squeals Sammy.

"Why did she stop?" asks Mark.

We hear another cheer and look back to see the JFK girl coming out from behind the gym. There's a Hampton girl behind her.

"They're going to pass her!" yells Wes.

"Heather, go!" I shout.

"Heather! You've got to get going!" screams Mark. "They're going to catch you!"

Everybody is cheering so loud, maybe she can't hear us. Or maybe she knows the other girls are coming and for once she doesn't care.

The JFK girl gives Heather a confused look as she races past, using the last of her energy to head for the chute and the finish line. The Hampton girl passes her, too. And then I see Heather's dad kiss her on the head and say something, and she nods and wipes her eyes and that's when she sees the green jerseys. Three Brockton girls are coming fast.

They pick up their pace, thinking they can get past her, but they don't know Heather. Once she's made up her mind, she takes off, and it's like she's flying, heading for the finish.

Suddenly, she looks like the Heather I know.

Or, maybe, like the Heather I knew.

CHAPTER 27

I WAIT WITH THE OTHER LAKEVIEW BOYS FOR the rest of the girls' team. Teresa and Victoria aren't too far back, and it's just a few more minutes before we see Brianne and Erica. We give them a cheer and watch as they gather together on the finish line side of the field.

I hear the ref's whistle. "Seventh-grade boys, ten minutes!" he announces. My stomach lurches. My head is filled with the shouts and cheers of the girls' race, and I feel like I've already run ten races today. I go over to my backpack, taking some deep breaths. I reach into the side pocket for my earplugs.

They're gone.

I look in the main compartment, digging way down deep, but they're not there. I check all the side pockets again. I know I put them there. I know it. My hands are starting to shake and I have that panicky feeling I get when everything is going wrong.

I hear a snort of laughter and look up. Two of the Brockton boys are watching me. When they see me look their way, they turn and make a big show of holding in their laughter in that

way that makes it even worse. Then I see a third Brockton kid coming over to me. I recognize him now for sure. It's the kid who pushed Heather.

"What's up?" he says. "Lose something?"

"My earplugs," I say. "I put them here in my backpack."

He opens his hand, holding out two mangled wads of green plastic. "Aw, I'm sorry," he says in that way that means just the opposite. "They must've fallen out. I thought they were gum." Then he drops them at my feet. "Tasted nasty." He starts to turn away, but changes his mind. "Bad day in the laundry room?" he asks. He reaches out to touch my singlet and I swat his hand away. "Hey, sorry," he says, pretending to be offended. "Well, you have a good race, bro."

He trots off to join the rest of the Brockton team.

I reach down and pick up the chewed earplugs. They're all pitted and covered in dirt. I squeeze them in my fist and lift my arm to throw them back down when I feel a hand on my shoulder. I jump and turn.

"Grandpa!" I say.

"You haven't run already, have you? I didn't miss it?"

"No, no, you didn't miss it," I mumble.

I'm trying to hold it in, but when I look at Grandpa's worried face, it all catches up with me: the earplugs, the race, Heather. It's not fair that she might go away, while kids like the ones from Brockton never do. You can shake Charlie

Kastner, but some Brockton kid will take his place. You could even lose the Brockton kid, and somebody new would show up. They multiply, and they find you, and they always, always win.

"What's wrong?" asks Grandpa. "Your folks are on the way. Your dad's train . . ." I open my hand and show him the earplugs. "What are those?"

"They were earplugs." I let them fall to the ground. "They're ruined. The ref fires a starting gun and without them I freeze, I can't even start." Then it all pours out of me. "And even if I run, I'll be terrible. Brockton will win, because they always do and I'll be last and I'll embarrass you and Mom and Dad, because I'm slow and I'll look stupid."

"Hey, slow down," says Grandpa.

"And Heather might be leaving—"

"Heather?"

"She's moving to Hawaii."

"Boys! Five minutes!" calls the ref.

"Okay," says Grandpa. "Listen, we'll talk about Heather later. Right now you have a race to run. Now, what's this about the starting gun?"

"It's too loud. I freak out."

"I think if you concentrate—"

"I can't! You don't understand! I can't do it without the earplugs!"

"You can, too. I know you can. You don't have to be afraid of it, Superhero."

That's when it explodes out of me. "I'm not a superhero!" I snap. "Stop calling me that! I am the complete, total opposite of a superhero!"

I've never yelled at Grandpa before. He looks surprised, but not angry. He grabs hold of both my shoulders and looks into my face. "Of course you are. You are a superhero." I try to pull away, but he holds me tight. "Listen. Why do you think you need the earplugs?"

"Because I'm afraid—"

"No! Because you hear more than other people. And you see more, and you feel so much more. That's the part of you that I love. You have all those superpowers. Why do you think I call you that?"

"I thought it was that Batman suit I used to wear."

"No! It's because of those beautiful, magical powers you have. Your super senses. And your super heart. That alone makes you a superhero."

"But the earplugs . . ."

"You can do it without them."

"I can't." Even as I say it, I picture Mrs. T's disappointed face.

"You can. Try. I know you can."

"I'm still going to be slow."

"What was that about a personal record you told me? What Mrs. R said?"

"Mrs. T—Coach T," I say.

"So that's what you're running for: a personal record."

"Seventh-grade boys, to the line!" calls the ref. I look over and see that everyone else is already there. I spot Lakeview's light blue jerseys. Sammy and Mark are looking around for me.

"Go on," says Grandpa. "I came to watch you run. Now go!"

I take a deep breath and go to the start. I squeeze in between Sammy and Sanjit. I can see that farther down the line the Brockton guys are already throwing jabs with their elbows to get the center position.

"We thought you weren't coming!" says Sanjit. He sounds relieved.

"I lost my earplugs," I say.

"Oh, man. Guys!" Sanjit pulls Mark over. "He lost his earplugs."

"Get him in the middle," says Mark. "He doesn't have his earplugs."

Sammy and Wes slide in on one side of me and Sanjit and Mark go on the other. "Don't worry," Sanjit tells me. "You're coming with us. Just hang on."

"Boys, ready!" calls the ref.

I put my hands over my ears. The guys press together

around me. I feel them on either side. I try not to shake too obviously and to keep breathing.

"Set!" calls the ref. I press on my ears as hard as I can.

BLAM!

I feel myself moving forward, but it's sort of like my body is leading and my legs are just keeping up. I realize that Sanjit has his arm through mine and Sammy has the other one and they're not letting me go. It's a sea of pounding feet and flying elbows. I swear I can feel the earth shake underneath us, and I run as fast as I can.

When they're sure I'm steady, they unwind their arms from mine. Somehow, I manage to keep up and we stay in a shaky pack, even though some kid steps on the back of Sanjit's foot and his shoe is half off. Wes is muttering something about throwing up. We're keeping up a decent pace, but way up ahead, Brockton is cruising in the lead—no surprise.

The whole Brockton team slips into the woods way before the rest of the teams, who have to fight for position. There are at least five teams bunched up and one little trail opening to fit into. It's a stomping, crazed race to get there. Our pack stays together, and we manage to get in ahead of JFK, but Hampton pushes in front of us at the last minute. We've all lost time in the shuffle for position, unlike the Brockton guys who are probably through the woods already and halfway up White Oak Lane.

When we're finally in the woods, everyone slows down. I know we have to pace ourselves and hold steady. The hill comes after the woods, then the trail behind the gym, and then we'll do it all over again.

In the woods, there's only the sound of runners: thumping feet, the huff and puff of our breathing. I just keep moving, following Mark and Sammy, being careful not to trip, as we wind our way through the trail to White Oak Lane. I think back to the first time I ran in these woods, sitting in the fallen leaves, pinned to a bush, and Heather coming back to find me. I remember how much I wanted to quit, how I would have quit, if it wasn't for her. And now she might be leaving and I'll be on my own again.

A few of the coaches are positioned on White Oak to stop traffic, so we don't get mowed down by unsuspecting parents coming to pick up their kids. When we come out on the road, I look up the hill. It's dotted with runners. I see every color jersey except for Brockton green. I guess those guys are already up the hill and on the trail behind the gym.

Everybody's grumbling. It's too steep. It's not fair. But to us it's just White Oak Lane, the hill we've run a million times. Even though I feel like I'm creeping along, I'm actually passing a couple of guys. Coach T told us it would be our friend. Now I understand what she meant.

Way in the distance, I can hear someone call "Brockton!"

They must be racing toward the woods for their second loop.

Wes looks like those chips were a big mistake, but he's digging in, still moving. Sanjit got his shoe back on. Our team is spread out, each of us going at his own pace. I'm almost up the hill, and for a second I feel relaxed, like maybe this will all come to a good end.

But then I hear another cheer. The Brockton boys are coming out of the woods and starting up White Oak for their second time. They know they're in the lead, and nobody can catch them, but now they're racing each other to finish first.

I turn onto the trail that goes behind the gym. It's just runners back here. There's no room for spectators, no coaches or parents, until the point when we come around the corner of the gym. It's a narrow trail, no space for packing up, hardly room for passing.

I hear footsteps and glance over my shoulder to see who's coming. It's the Brockton kid. The one who ruined my earplugs. The one who pushed Heather. I'm still huffing and puffing from the hill, but I stay in the middle of the trail. I hate the fact that he's coming up behind me, that even on his second loop, he's going to catch me.

The footsteps get closer and I feel an elbow. It's him.

"Get out of the way," he says.

Before I know what I'm doing, I jab him back. I remember

those fast little steps from the fartleks, and I pick up the pace so he can't pass.

"Get out of the way, stupid," he says. "You still mad about the ear things?"

"No," I say. "Heather."

"What?" he says.

"The last meet," I gasp. This is way faster than I'm used to going. "Last meet you pushed my friend."

"You mean a push like this?" he says. I know it's coming, so I somehow duck under his elbow, just missing being bounced off the back wall of the gym like a pinball.

I've slowed us down enough so that the other Brockton runners are catching up. "You're"—gasp—"a cheater." I say it loud enough so the others can hear.

"What's up, Trey?"

"Nothing," Trey says. "This kid won't move."

"The last"—choke—"meet," I gasp. "He pushed a girl and she sprained . . ." I don't have enough breath to finish, but they get the point.

"Trey, you pushed a girl?" one of the guys says.

"No, I didn't," Trey says.

"Did," I say.

"She tripped."

"Elbowed," I say. My legs are killing me, but I have to keep blocking him.

"She was in my way," says Trey.

"You couldn't pass a girl?" says another kid.

"Not"—gasp—"this"—choke—"girl," I say.

"You're an idiot, Trey."

We're almost at the end of the trail, and I know the coaches and parents will be positioned to see who's coming out first. I know that Trey has had enough of me. I know he's itching to go. But I hold my ground in the middle of the trail, my legs shaky. As we come to the corner of the building, I slow down, just a little. Just enough. I feel his elbow in my armpit and this time I don't fight it. I couldn't even if I wanted to. I feel the shove and just as we come around the corner, out into the open, I'm jolted up in the air.

It feels like I'm up there for a long time—long enough to see parents dressed in Brockton green, and some with their faces painted Hampton orange. There are people in Lakeview blue and Fox Ridge purple. Coming down, I see the shock on their faces, the Brockton coach's face most of all. And as I finally land on my rear in a stinky, wet cushion of leaves, I think to myself: *Mission accomplished.*

CHAPTER 28

ONE OF THE OTHER BROCKTON RUNNERS STOPS and helps me up. He's shaking his head and looking ahead at Trey, who's raced off to finish. The Brockton coach is writing something on his clipboard. I hear Sammy's voice, "Joseph, get up, come on," and then he's pulling me up, too. A few runners pass by, a few fast kids on their second loop, but most are still on their first, like me.

I brush the dirt off my knees. One is scraped and a little bloody, but I don't care.

"Joseph!" It's Heather, calling from the crowd. Even from a distance, I can tell that she saw it all. Finally, I've paid her back. "Personal record!" she calls. "Bring it home!"

I'm still shaken up, but before any more runners can pass me, I stumble to my feet and start running on the strip of field that leads back to the woods. I'm starting to understand what it means to be on your last legs, but everybody's watching and I can't quit now. I keep going until I stumble into the woods, and the cheers of the crowd disappear.

It's quiet again. We're all spread out, no more packs, just

runners, each one of us trying not to give up. It's cool and shaded and I look at the trees around me, bouncing and blurry as I run. The trail stretches out ahead, and a squirrel dashes across it, looking edgy and upset by all these kids coming from who-knows-where. I hear the crinkle of leaves underfoot and the vague huffing sound of another runner behind me. I keep trudging.

After all the action and the cheers, it's amazingly peaceful here. My mind says, *Keep going, keep going.* My body is shouting, *What, are you crazy?* But for once I have no energy for worrying. I just have to finish.

When I get to White Oak Lane, I'm back in the sun and I stare up the hill. I remember the first time I climbed it, the stitch in my side, gravity pulling me down. Even though I'm stronger and fitter and I've done it a million times, it's still steep and I'm still tired and I still wonder if I can make it.

But I put one foot in front of the other, and I see Sammy and Wes at the top of the hill. Somewhere along the way, Wes must have picked it up. I think about who's waiting for me: Heather. Coach T. Grandpa. Maybe my parents have even made it. I think about finishing. I think about a personal record.

I finally make it to the trail behind the gym. There isn't far to go now. This time there are no Brockton runners. They all finished a long time ago. I know the crowd is waiting, and I wish I could smile as I turn the corner, but everything hurts, especially the hip I landed on and my knee. I just have to concentrate on making it to the chute and then to the finish line.

I hear Grandpa's voice first: "You're almost there, Joseph!"

And Heather's: "Finish strong!"

And then a chorus of girls' voices: "Go, Joseph! Looking good!"

"Go get 'em, Joseph!" calls another voice. It's Mrs. Fishbein! I'd forgotten all about Mrs. Fishbein!

Up ahead I can see Sammy and Wes. They're crossing the finish line. There are a couple of kids in front of me, and they look even worse than I feel. I find one last, painful burst of energy and push as hard as I've ever pushed myself to pass them. I race to the finish line, stumble across, and tumble to the ground.

Coach T is jumping up and down and clapping her hands. George and Ringo pounce on me, covering me with bulldog snorts. Wes is pointing back to the course, where Mark and Sanjit are finishing. I manage to pull myself up to cheer them home. They cross the line and then we're all catching our breath, watching, amazed, as maybe twenty-five kids finish after us. Twenty-five runners, maybe more! After us!

Sanjit brings me over a cup of Gatorade and my hand is shaking so hard I can barely drink it. The girls are all on the other side of the field, waiting for the signal that all the boys are through so they can cross back over to join us at the finish.

But all the boys aren't through. In the distance there's a lone figure coming out from behind the gym, wobbling his way toward us. It's Heber. All the spectators are too busy gathering their stuff and looking for their kids to even bother with a pity cheer.

I somehow make my legs move, and I pull Sanjit and Mark with me.

"Heber!" I call to him. I try to give him the most unpitying cheer I can think of. "You're not looking good. You look terrible. Awful! But you're going to finish. You're going to finish! You can do it."

Then Sammy and Wes join in, and Heber's teammates come over, too.

"You can do it, Heber!" they call out. "Finish strong!"

There's not much change in Heber's stride. He just keeps chugging along, but his face brightens and his eyebrows scrunch together, and he keeps moving. Barely, but he keeps moving. We follow him to the finish chute. It's slow going, but we're with him, step for lumbering step.

When he finally crosses the finish line, we all break into cheers.

"Way to go! PR! PR!" we cheer, even though we have no idea if he PRed or not.

I'm suddenly aware that I can't move another inch. I don't think I have the strength to lower myself to the ground, but I can't stay up, either.

The girls have gotten the signal that they can cross the field, and soon every girl on every team is heading toward us in a wave.

"Wow," says Sammy. "It's like a dream come true."

Soon they're surrounding us and there are high fives and hand slaps and lots of jumping around. Erica rushes over to Sanjit and hugs him around the waist. He looks surprised and then he smiles really wide. I think he finally gets it.

Then, all of a sudden I'm being picked up and spun around.

"Great race, Friedman! You did it!" It's a little embarrassing to be so easily hoisted in the air, but Heather looks so proud of me, I don't really mind. She puts me down and now I'm not only tired and shaky, but dizzy, too. I lie down on the grass and Heather sits next to me. She starts talking right away.

"You PR'd for sure. Isn't it the best feeling ever?"

I hardly have breath enough to answer. "Yuh," I say with a nod.

She lowers her voice a little and says, "And that move with Trey."

"Who?" I say. My mind is a blur.

"Trey, the Brockton kid. You timed it perfectly," she whispers. "Don't you want to know what happened to him?"

"Why?" I ask. "Did he get in trouble?"

"He was DQ'd," says Heather.

It takes every ounce of energy I have left to raise my head two inches and ask, "Dairy Queened?"

"Disqualified," she explains, letting a smile spread across her face.

I get a surge of strength and sit up straight. "Disqualified?!"

"Unsportsmanlike conduct."

"Really?" I say.

"Are you kidding? They'd have to be blind not to see that elbow."

Coach T's voice comes over the loudspeaker. "Awards in ten minutes! Everyone over to the finish line. Awards in ten!"

I guess I have to get over there, if for no other reason than Coach T says so. But there's the question of moving. I'm trying to figure out how I'm going to make it from sitting all the way to standing. I'm about to give it my best shot when Heather says, "Hold on. I have to tell you something."

And then it all comes rushing back. How Heather might be moving. How she hugged her father, the sign he gave, the way she was crying.

"I talked to my mom today," says Heather.

"Today? I thought she was calling—"

"Tonight. I know, but . . . I couldn't think of anything but her. I couldn't concentrate. Have you ever felt like that? Like you just can't focus?"

"Like every day?" I say.

"Oh. Yeah." She covers her mouth, trying to hide her smile. I guess for a minute there she forgot who she was talking to. "So, with the race today and everything . . . I couldn't wait till tonight. I left school early and we called her. We talked. My mom, my dad, and me."

"What did you say?" I ask, but I'm thinking, *Please stay. Please, please stay.*

"I told her the truth, like you said. I told her how much I liked it here and how I don't want to move again. But I said if the only way we could be together was for us to move to Hawaii, then I'd do it."

I don't say anything, but I realize if it was me, if it was the only way I could be with my mom and dad, that would be the truth for me, too.

"We talked about everything. We really, really talked. It sounds weird, but we never did that before. She told me things I never knew. How she got to be a scientist. How she never even liked being Blueberry Princess."

"She didn't?"

"No! She just did it to make her mom happy. She told me how much she missed being with me and Dad. Then I told her stuff and she listened. I told her about school and

my drawings and the team. I told her stuff about being...
me."

"Awards, ladies and gentlemen, in five minutes!" calls
Coach T. "At the finish!"

"So—" I start.

"So, when I left, my mom and dad were still talking.
They needed to work things out, too. But I felt like whatever
happened, somehow things were better. Somehow, it would
be okay. And I got here just in time."

"But you didn't know if you were staying or ..."

She shakes her head. "Not until I saw my dad."

"Doing this." I imitate what her dad did with his hands.

She smiles. "The baseball sign. It's the sign for home. If
you're on third base it means, 'Run home.'"

I still don't get it.

"My mom's coming home."

When I hear that I feel like I could bounce to my feet in a
single jump. In reality, though, I push off and fall right back
down again.

"We're going to Hawaii for Christmas," Heather says,
laughing at me. "She'll show us the *Hibiscus waimeae* and the
orchids and the rainbows, but then she'll come home with
us." She leans over and plucks a last little clover flower out of
the grass and twirls it between her fingers. "She'll still travel.
She has to. But she wants to spend more time with me. She

wants to see me run. I told her about Lakeview, how much I like it here. Even with Charlie Kastner and those Brockton guys. Even with the fartleks."

Maybe it's just the nervous energy and all the stuff I've been holding in, but when she says "fartleks" I can't stop laughing and neither can she. I'm so overloaded with fatigue and confusion and relief, it's like ten starting guns are going off over my head.

Heather holds out her hand. I remember that time in the woods back in September when she freed me from the thorn-bush. Now I take her hand and she pulls me up like I don't weigh an ounce.

"Come on," she says. "Awards." She starts off toward the group that's gathering around the finish line.

"So you're okay with third place?" I ask her as I limp beside her. My legs still aren't working so well.

She thinks for a second, then says, "I like winning. But there are other things that matter, too. Sometimes they matter more. Today, that's how it was. So, yeah. I'm okay with third place. I'll get 'em next time."

Grandpa comes over and rumples my hair. I guess he was giving me some time with Heather. "Well done, Superhero. And Heather, you run like a gazelle."

"Ostrich, more like," she says.

"Is everything..." Grandpa looks from me to Heather and back again.

"She's staying," I say, and I can't help grinning.

I see Mrs. Fishbein looking a little lost over by an oak tree. "Come here, Grandpa," I say. "There's someone I want you to meet." Heather comes, too, and I use what's left of my energy to hobble over to Mrs. Fishbein.

"Joseph!" she says. "I never knew running could be so exciting. That Heber fellow seems to be a crowd favorite."

"Mrs. Fishbein," I say. "I want you to meet my grandfather. He doesn't like liquid soap or golf. But he likes Italian opera. Grandpa, this is Mrs. Fishbein, our librarian. She doesn't like computers or scanners. She loves an island called Inishbofin."

Grandpa smiles and Mrs. Fishbein says, "It's nice to meet an opera lover. I thought my parrot, Luciano, and I were the last ones."

"A Pavarotti fan, are you?" Grandpa asks.

"Yes, are you?"

"Well, of course," he says. "Though my favorite might be Corelli . . ."

"Ah. A Radamès to die for," answers Mrs. Fishbein.

"Aida thought so, too," says Grandpa.

I don't have a clue who Corelli is, or Radamès, either, but they both seem to find this incredibly funny.

We hear a whistle, and Coach T's voice comes through a megaphone. "Seventh-grade awards ceremony, at the finish line. All seventh-grade teams to the finish line now, please! Eighth graders are waiting to run."

Grandpa and Mrs. Fishbein keep talking. I hear her say, "Kids don't even know what they think until they text their friends." And Grandpa says something about rap music and George Gershwin that makes her laugh.

I look at Heather. She's trying to hide a grin. I think it's time for us to get going.

"Grandpa, I'll see you later," I say. "There's an awards thing over at the finish line." He gives me a thumbs-up, but I don't know if he really heard me.

Heather and I make our way across the track to join the rest of the team.

"Why do we have to watch the awards?" grumbles Sammy. "Brockton's going to get all of them."

"Hey, they're not all so bad," I say. "One of them stopped to help me up."

"And the first ten finishers get medals," says Brianne. "So Heather will get one."

"Yeah, be polite," adds Victoria, and she gives Sammy a nudge, which he doesn't seem to mind.

Coach T and the ref are consulting a clipboard and a timer. Finally, Coach T looks up and calls out, "Okay, great meet today! Thank you all for coming to Lakeview. We'll start with girls' top ten finishers." She calls out the girls' names, and they go up for their medals. She tries not to change her voice when she calls Heather's name, but I can hear how proud she is.

There are two team awards, and the Brockton girls get first place and JFK gets second.

When the boys' medals are announced, I watch all the Brockton boys go up one by one. All except Trey. I get some satisfaction from that. There are a couple of JFK runners mixed into the top ten, one from Hampton, and one from St. Aloysius.

Of course Brockton gets team first place, and one of their guys takes the medals and tosses them around like they're hot potatoes. I'm about to go find Grandpa and Mrs. Fishbein, when I hear Coach T say, "Boys' second place team medal goes to . . ." and then she calls out, "Lakeview!"

We look at each other and nobody moves.

"Come on up and get your medals, Lakeview!"

Sammy moves first, sprinting over to Coach T, and then the others follow him, but I'm too amazed to move. How could that be? How could we be second? Out of all those teams, how could we have come in second?

When the guys come back, everybody's jumping around and giving high fives. Sanjit puts a medal in my hand. "Take it, Joseph, it's yours."

I stare down at it. It's not like those phony plastic medals that are painted gold and start to chip the day you get them.

It's heavy and it's made of metal and it hangs by a red, white, and blue ribbon.

I hear the ref call the eighth-grade girls to the line. Coach T is back with us, grabbing us all for a group hug.

"You didn't cheat to get us this, did you?" I ask her.

"Joseph! How could I cheat?" she says. "We added up the numbers."

"But none of us were even in the top ten."

"It doesn't matter," she says. "It's the total score of the top five runners on each team. Some schools didn't even have five. Kids dropped off, gave up. We let kids race, but without five, they couldn't score as a team. Some schools had two fast runners, but the others were way back. Some guys quit when they saw the hill. When we added everything up, Brockton was first and you guys were second." She holds up three fingers. "Girl Scout's honor."

"And you were blazing!" Mark says to me. "Maybe we should thank that Brockton dude for making you go so fast."

Heather takes the medal and puts it around my neck. She's already wearing hers.

That's when my mom and dad show up. Dad is catching his breath. He's pointing up to the parking lot and pantomiming that he ran all the way.

My mother looks at my medal. "Second place! Joseph! I never thought . . . we never thought . . ."

"Oh, it was even more exciting than that," says Coach T.

Poor Dad looks like he might keel over. "I'm sorry"—gasp—"we're late" —gasp—"the train was stopped." That's all he can manage to say, but I'm so happy to see them. They tried so hard, it hardly matters that they missed the race.

"Take it easy, Dad," I say. "You can come watch me run in winter, or spring. Grandpa saw it all. He'll tell you about it."

"Where is Grandpa?" Mom asks.

I point up to the tree where I left him with Mrs. Fishbein. Grandpa is leaning against the tree, looking so cool he could almost be a high school kid.

"Who's that with him?" asks my mother.

"Mrs. Fishbein, the librarian," I say. Mom looks at me like she wonders if I had anything to do with this. I'll tell her sometime.

"I don't want to interrupt," she says. "I think Grandpa can find his way home. Do you want a ride?"

"Um, I'd kind of like to hang out here for a while, if that's okay," I say. "Stretch, cool down, watch the eighth-grade race. I can walk home."

"Of course."

"Just take care of Dad," I say. Mom smiles, and after a bunch of hugs, I watch my father limp back to the parking lot.

When they go, I hold the medal in my hand and feel its weight. It's heavy and solid and real.

I think about the Friedman Law of Worry: There will always be something you don't think of. And that's what will get you. But that's okay. Because you'll get through it and then something else will happen. And something else. And you'll get through that, too. And then one day there'll be something you didn't think of that gets you, and you'll realize, it's the best thing ever.

I lie down on my back and look up at the sky. I feel my medal on my chest. I watch the clouds pass and I feel the afternoon breeze and the sun shines down on me. Joseph Friedman. Lakeview Leopard. Cross country medalist.

EPILOGUE

EVER SINCE HEATHER PUNCHED OUT CHARLIE, he's pretty much been leaving us alone. It sort of calls into question that "Use your words" rule everybody's been telling us since nursery school. Still, a lot of other things can happen when you punch somebody in the face, so I guess it's still a good rule of thumb to use your words, when possible.

In PE, we've moved from soccer to softball to kickball, and sometimes badminton when the weather is bad. Badminton is the only one I relax in, because no matter how hard somebody hits that little birdie at you, it still can't do too much damage.

But today, Coach DeSalvo announces that we're going to run.

"Okay, ladies and gentlemen," he says, as we gather on the track. "We have this new track, so it's about time we used it. We're going to run a mile today. Now, I said run, not race. I want everybody to be smart about this. Go your own pace. Now, we have a couple of cross country runners here—"

Charlie coughs into his hand something that sounds like "nerds," but Coach DeSalvo ignores him.

"—so you might want to take a page from their book and take it easy. No sprinting. It's four laps around. Save something for the last two laps. So, let's line up, and when I blow the whistle, go."

As we line up, I remember that first PE class on the soccer field, when I first saw Heather.

So much has changed since then.

Heather is going to Hawaii in December, and when she comes home, she'll be together with her mom and dad. Grandpa has actually gone to Sunshine Senior Living to visit Eddie, and last night the two of them went to the Metropolitan Opera . . . along with Mrs. Fishbein!

Last week I got my research paper back and I got a B. I wrote about a marathon runner named Meb Keflezighi, who grew up in Africa, became an American citizen, and won the New York and Boston Marathons—after he broke his hip and could barely walk. One of my sources was a book that I found in the library that he wrote himself. Its Dewey Decimal number is 796.42K. Mr. Hernandez is a pretty strict teacher, but when I explained that Meb is just known as "Meb" and hardly anybody uses his last name, he surprised me and let me just write *Meb* instead of spelling out *Keflezighi* each time.

As Coach DeSalvo puts the whistle in his mouth, I look

around. The trees have leaves of orange and yellow and even some tips of red; the breeze has a winter chill. A squirrel pokes around under the bleachers. He's digging furiously, trying to bury a fat old acorn. When the whistle blows, the squirrel takes off.

So does Charlie. He's about three kids away from me and he's out like a flash. "See you later, dork," he calls back to me. Billy and Zachary are right on his heels. They're going really fast. I'd like to warn them, but then again, I wouldn't.

Heather bounds off, but not as fast as Charlie, who looks over his shoulder and smirks. I start slow. I'm still feeling it from the meet, and besides, I'm not out to prove anything.

Coach DeSalvo is calling out, "Take it easy, boys, you have four laps to run," but of course Charlie and his friends don't listen. They're sprinting through the first lap, racing each other, shoving and laughing. I know they're going to pass me, and when I hear them coming I move to the outside of the track and let them go by.

"Looking good!" I say cheerily. Charlie gives me a suspicious glare, but not surprisingly, he doesn't have a lot of breath left to answer.

Heather passes a second later and we exchange a glance. We both know it won't be long now.

Looking across the track, I can see that Charlie and his buddies are slowing down. They try to make it look like they're just relaxing, but I know that's not it. Heather passes them easily, and then she accelerates. I'm feeling pretty good, and I start to pick up my pace. The track feels solid under my feet, so easy after running over tree roots and up hills. I'm already looking forward to winter track, when we run indoors. I can't imagine—a whole track inside a building! And spring track and field, running right here, and watching Heather throw discus.

Now I'm gaining on Charlie and he's rubbing his side. The stitch has struck. I try not to smile as I pass him and his buddies, who are stumbling along beside him. I watch Heather blaze around her last lap, a blur of limbs and energy and crazy, windblown hair. It's no surprise that she finishes first.

I don't blaze, but I finish feeling pretty good, almost a full lap ahead of Charlie, who is clutching his side and limping along until he finally crosses the finish line and sits down in the middle of the center lane, trying to catch his breath.

I realize that we could laugh at him. We could say, "Ha, ha, who's a wimp now?" We could hold our arms up and jump up and down and sing, "We Are the Champions." We could do a million things.

I look over at Heather. She motions with her head, letting me do the honors.

I walk over to Charlie Kastner and say, "It's okay. You went out too fast and got a stitch. It happened to me, too, at first."

He's looking up at me, and I know he wants to say something mean, but before he can, I reach out my hand. He looks over and sees that Coach DeSalvo is watching. So is everybody else.

I guess there's a line that even bullies know not to cross: the line that puts you into sore loser territory, where you become just a stupid pile of loser muscle. So when he takes my hand, he doesn't pull me to the ground, even though he probably could. It's not easy, but I manage to use some leverage and get him to his feet. I can tell his side is still hurting.

"Have a banana," I say. "For the stitch." Then I add, "Potassium."

Coach DeSalvo comes over and puts his hands on our shoulders. "I'm glad to see you two getting along," he says, "because Coach Papasian tells me Charlie's going to be joining you for indoor track over the winter."

I look at Charlie, who doesn't seem all that pleased with the arrangement.

"Shot put, right, Charlie?"

Charlie nods.

I look at Heather, and she's covering her face with her hands. When she takes them down, she's grinning.

It should be an interesting winter.

ACKNOWLEDGMENTS

I'd like to start by acknowledging the teachers who started me on the road to becoming a writer: Ms. Akers, Ms. Johnston, Mr. Benjamin, Mr. Gordon, Mr. Giamatti, I am forever grateful.

It was a happy day when Nicole James agreed to be my agent. And things only got better when Erica Finkel became my editor. I'm so grateful to the whole wonderful team at Abrams, and to Anne Heltzel, for finding that perfect word I was searching for. Thank you all for believing in Joseph and Heather, and in me.

A thousand hugs to MacKenzie Cadenhead and Jessica Benjamin, my writing buddies, and to Alyssa Capucilli, who brought us together. I could not have made this book what it is without your advice, encouragement and, most of all, your friendship.

My endless gratitude to the original Mrs. T, and to all of the teachers, coaches, teammates, parents, grandparents and friends who make us into superheroes. And a special thank you to Bobby Asher, and to all the crazy, devoted runners of the world, who continue to amaze and inspire me.

Love and thanks to my mother and father, who gave me a childhood of safety, laughter, and kindness, and to my sister, Marcie, who blazed every trail, making each step of growing up a little easier.

And finally, all my love to my husband, Henry, and our sons, Bobby, Benjy, and Adam. You make me feel proud and loved, and like the luckiest person in the world, every single day.

ABOUT THE AUTHOR

Diana Harmon Asher is the mother of three sons. She lives with her husband, Henry, in Westchester, New York, and spends her days writing, teaching, volunteering, and conversing with their dog, Cody, and cat, Chester. *Sidetracked* is her debut novel.

AUTHOR Q&A

An interview with **Diana Harmon Asher**

1. How did you come up with the idea for *Sidetracked*, and for your main character, Joseph?

One of the things that I love about the sport of cross country is how it can turn the most unlikely athletes into runners. Joseph sees himself as the worst athlete on the planet, and joining a sports team is the last thing he expects to happen in seventh grade. I wanted to tell the story from Joseph's point of view, to portray the world as he saw and felt it—including the anxieties, the confusions, and self-doubt. As I wrote, Joseph developed a unique personality, with lots of peculiarities, but lots of strengths, too. When Heather and Grandpa entered the storyline, I realized that a theme common to all of them was the way expectations weigh us all down. I tried to write a story that showed each of them trying to reconcile who they are with what they are expected to be.

2. Did you know how the novel would end before you started writing it, or did you make many changes along the way?

That's a really interesting question. I knew that I wanted Joseph to grow, and to have a victory, but in a realistic way. I didn't want him to join the team and suddenly discover a hidden athletic talent that makes him "okay." But I also didn't want to give him some consolation prize, like a sportsmanship award. He needed to come through for Heather, and also prove something to himself, but he had to do it using the traits we've seen in him throughout the story, and what he's learned from Coach T and his teammates. I've been to a lot of meets (all three of my sons ran cross country), and it's common for the faster runners to "lap," or overtake the slower runners. That gave me a chance to have Joseph cross paths with faster runners during the final meet, but it took a while to figure out exactly what would happen there. I also went to a middle-school league meet to cheer on a team that my son was coaching. Watching the finish, I realized that there are ways to earn a "win" while still not being anywhere near the fastest one out there.

3. Why did you choose running as the focus of the book?

Cross country and track-and-field are sports that take in all those kids who have been cut from basketball, soccer, baseball. A lot of kids' hearts are broken around seventh grade, when they're told they can't play those sports for their school. Cross country and track is where they find their "team." There are also some really terrific athletes—boys and girls—who choose cross country and track, so there's a great mix of talents and abilities. I also love the concept of the PR—the Personal Record. The idea of "doing your best" is great, but trying for a Personal Record is more than that. It means that your goal is to improve, to resist the urge to quit, to persevere and do better than you did last time. There's nothing wrong with competing with others—racing can be incredibly exciting! But for a kid like Joseph, striving for a PR can be so important, as a place to start. I have to admit, I also saw so many comic possibilities in the sport—goose poop on the track, mud on the trails, tiny little running shorts. And really, who can resist writing about a sport that has a term like "fartlek?"

4. Nothing is going right for Joseph until Mrs. T inspires and pushes him. Did you have a teacher like that?

When I wrote the acknowledgments for *Sidetracked*, I realized that the first people I had to thank were my favorite teachers— from elementary school all the way through college. They were kind, creative, and supportive. In fact, I sent my first- and fifth-grade teachers an early reading copy of the book, and it was an incredible experience to reconnect with them. That said, my needs were very different from Joseph's. Unlike Joseph, academics and school life came easily to me.

The teacher who encourages Joseph—Mrs. T—was actually inspired by one of the incredible resource room teachers in my sons' school—Nancy Tannenbaum. She was quite a character—loving, talented, and feisty. She understood kids like Joseph. They were "her" kids, and she would fight for them like a mother tiger protecting her cubs. Sadly, she passed away a few years ago, but her students and their parents will never forget her. I think she would have recognized parts of herself in *Sidetracked*'s "Mrs. T," and I hope she would have loved her as much as I do.

5. What was your process for capturing a seventh-grade boy's inner thoughts?

One of my writing workshop buddies recently pointed out how much I'm like Joseph. I don't have ADD, I'm not a seventh-grade boy, I didn't really have trouble making friends. But I do worry a lot, and I guess I observe things in a very particular way. When Charlie's football cleat lands on the bee, for instance, Joseph's reaction is exactly how I would react. Poor bee! Is it squashed? Is it trapped? Can I save it? Please, let it be okay. I guess I just extended that thinking through the lens of Joseph's personality. I'm also the mother of three sons, and I've tried to be around and involved, and to listen a lot. So, in an odd way, I felt right at home in the hallways and sports fields of middle school.

6. What do you hope that a reader of *Sidetracked* who does not have ADD will get from your book (besides an entertaining read)?

I hope the book will make readers think about giving other people a chance—and giving themselves a chance. ADD is just a part of Joseph. There are so many quirks, differences and talents that make each person unique. Joseph is more self-aware than most kids, and maybe readers will look at their own challenges, try to understand them, and even laugh a little bit. I hope they will get the message that you can see humor in just about any situation. I also hope that readers will think about society's expectations of gender, physical appearance, and success. And yes, I hope they are entertained, and finish the book smiling.

7. What are you working on now?

I'm working on another middle-grade novel, this time told from a girl's point of view. I don't want to say too much about it, because I'm still working it out, but it moves from the world of middle-school running to the world of middle-school musical theater.

8. Anything else we should know?

This is my first published novel, and I've been waiting and working for a long, long time. It's hard to convey how much it means to me that *Sidetracked* has gotten such an enthusiastic reception. I've spoken with kids who tell me they trudged through their summer reading assignments, then they flew through *Sidetracked* and really loved it. Hearing that just warms my heart.

Author Q&A courtesy of Dave Shallenberger, co-owner of Little Shop of Stories (Decatur, Georgia); Bookselling This Week, a publication of the American Booksellers Association; and Deborah Kalb of deborahkalbbooks.blogspot.com.

DISCUSSION QUESTIONS FOR *SIDETRACKED*

1. What comparison does Joseph make to describe his middle-school experience? What does he convey with that comparison?

2. How can we describe the reactions to Heather in the first three chapters? How does her being a girl impact the way people react to her?

3. What challenges do we learn that Joseph and Heather have in common? How are their challenges different?

4. Why is it difficult for Joseph to form friendships, even with others who are trying to be kind to him?

5. Based on Joseph's description at the beginning of Chapter 6, how would you describe Mrs. Fishbein? What does she have in common with Joseph?

6. How do Joseph's classmates generally perceive what he is doing in school? How does he explain what he is doing at those moments?

7. Throughout the book, what role do adults play in the social division that we see between groups of kids?

8. How does the author use sensory details to help tell the story? What purposes do these details serve?

9. What does Joseph mean when he says, "Maybe I've had enough years of personal defeat and I'm ready to give shared misery a try"? Why is "shared misery" appealing?

10. What's the importance of Mrs. T's quote, "Joseph did what Joseph could do today"?

11. How does the retirement home remind Joseph of middle school? Why does he say, "I've gotten to help Grandpa with his jailbreak after all"?

12. When Joseph wants to quit, what makes Heather's pep talk effective?

13. Why is the uniform so important to Joseph? What does it symbolize for him?

14. Throughout the book, what is it about running that gives Joseph a sense of belonging that he hadn't found before?

15. What are the different feelings that Joseph has about the encouragement he gets after his first race?

16. In Chapter 18, what is the "problem" that Joseph identifies about cross country as a sport? Do you see that as a problem?

17. What is the significance of Heather's name? How does it fit her personality?

18. Why does Heather talk to Joseph the way she does at the Brockton meet?

19. How do Joseph and Heather each show a different side of themselves at the league meet?

20. How does Grandpa explain Joseph's reaction to the gun? How does this explanation help Joseph see himself differently?

21. What do Joseph's actions at the end of the book show us about him as a person?

READ ON FOR A SAMPLE OF DIANA HARMON ASHER'S NEXT BOOK, *UPSTAGED!*

Chapter 1

Pilgrim Feet

The front hallway of Hedgebrook Middle School has that slippery, early morning shine. I know by the end of the day it'll be back to its usual self, gray and grubby, marked up with black sneaker skids and gum pies. But now it's still polished and new and dotted with sunny spotlights. I weave a path around them, zigzagging my way to Mr. Hoover's Music Appreciation class.

Cassie's already waiting in the doorway, bouncing on her toes and waving me in. She has a new streak in her hair, bright blue to match her glasses. "Come on, Shira! The announcement, remember?"

Of course I remember. Mr. Hoover is really into announcements, and he's already let it slip that today's announcement is going to be about the school musical.

There's no reason why I should feel nervous. I have first-period math and Ms. Jablonski's evil pop quiz safely behind me. And I want to hear about the musical. I do. But something's making me hover in the doorway, until finally

Cassie has to practically yank me off my feet and pull me inside. We plop down in the third row.

"I *cain't* wait," Cassie says, putting on the goofy twang the kids used in last year's musical. "I want to get dressed up all *purty*."

"And dance with a *feller*," I say, then I throw in, *"Yeehaw."*

To be honest, it wasn't the best production in history. A cardboard cutout horse crashed down, barely missing the leading lady. And at the end, somebody stepped on the kid playing a farmhand who was supposed to be dead ("daid"). He screamed—much louder than a dead person ever would. It pretty much killed the drama.

Still, all the girls looked nice in their fluffy skirts, and the boys got to act all country, in their cowboy boots and hats. And, I admit, I wondered how it would feel to be up there in a costume, holding hands, singing, and taking a bow.

Mr. Hoover claps his hands for quiet. He's looking spiffy, as always, in a light green striped button-down shirt, pressed and tucked neatly into his khaki pants.

"Okay," he calls out. "Settle down now, people. I have an announcement!"

A cry of "whoo-whoo" comes from the other side of the room. I poke Cassie in the ribs.

"So, who came to see last year's musical?" asks Mr. Hoover.

Cassie and I raise our hands high, then look around

and lower them slowly. We're either the only two who went, or the only two uncool enough to admit it.

"Well, it was amazing," Mr. Hoover continues. "And this year's is going to be just as great. Now, enough suspense," he says, as if we're all on the edges of our seats. "I'm happy to announce—that this year—our school musical—will be—*The Music Man!*"

Cassie and I look at each other, not sure if this is good news or bad.

"This is such a great show. It's about a lovable con man and a small-town librarian . . ."

A drawn-out yawn comes from somewhere, and in the row behind us, a boy named Eric starts manufacturing a lineup of spitballs. The excitement is dwindling fast.

"Now, wait a minute!" calls out Mr. Hoover. "Keep listening. Because this year, we're holding auditions right here in music class!"

"Whuh?" says somebody, eloquently speaking for all of us.

"We'll still have after-school auditions, but I'm opening up our class today to anyone who wants to sing."

"Wait," says Cassie. "Now?"

"Yes!" answers Mr. Hoover, looking delighted. "And I *know* you're not ready. But that's the thing! There's no time to get nervous, no time to talk yourself out of it. I want everyone to take a chance. Even if you've never been in a show. Even if you're really, really shy."

When he says that last part, I swear he's looking right at me.

"What do we sing?" asks a girl named Frankie.

"Anything! 'My Country 'Tis of Thee' or 'America the Beautiful,' or . . . 'Uptown Funk' . . ." He pauses, clearly expecting a laugh, but there's silence. "Then come by Thursday after school to read a few lines, and you're done!"

Mr. Hoover sits down at the piano and waves an arm. "So, line up and let's go!"

Two boys in front of me start pushing each other, racing to hide under their chairs. Eric drops his spitballs and bolts dramatically for the door.

I sit still in my seat.

"Come on," says Cassie. "Let's get in line."

"Are you *kidding*?" I answer.

"Why not? You're in chorus. You have a nice voice."

"That's different. You don't have to audition for chorus."

"You know, when he said that shy part, he was looking right at—"

"I know," I snap.

"Listen," says Cassie, "we can't possibly be worse than that."

She's talking about Kevin Clancy. He's the kid who always wants to go first—scoliosis screening, hearing test, it doesn't matter. He's singing, "My Country 'Tis of Thee." At least I think that's what it is.

Mr. Hoover congratulates Kevin. "See?" he says. "It's easy." A few more kids start to get in line.

Cassie is standing, hands on hips. "What happened to this being the year you were going to stop being Shy Shira? The year you were going to stop blushing at every little thing?"

I take this as a reminder not to share secret goals with anyone, even if they are your best friend.

"We can go after school," I mumble.

"You know you won't," she says, and she's right. I won't. "Look, if you don't audition, I won't, either. Then neither of us will be in the show, and I'll never let you forget it. Ever."

I know she's not bluffing. She'll blame me, forever.

So, when she pulls me up out of my chair, I let her, even though my knees are shaking, and I feel like I might end up "daid" on the music room floor. And when she goes to the back of the line, I stand behind her, holding on to the thought that Cassie will go first, then I can bail.

Meanwhile, a group of boys cracks up through "She'll Be Coming 'Round the Mountain," and then a girl starts "My Heart Will Go On," but she loses her way and ends up in "I Will Always Love You." Somehow, Mr. Hoover knows to go along with her.

I'm fourth in line and it feels like feeding time for the butterflies in my stomach.

None of this makes sense. The kids who get the good parts are the ones who take acting lessons and dance class and go to Rising Starz Music Camp. The outgoing kids, the ones with confidence. Not kids like Cassie and me.

I stare at the floor, the singing and giggling a blur around me. But when I look up, Cassie isn't in front of me anymore. She's singing an enthusiastic and slightly off-pitch verse of "Oh My Darling Clementine." And then, before I can think of where to hide, it's my turn.

"'America the Beautiful'?" Mr. Hoover suggests, and before I can say no, please no, he plays a note and smiles.

Not every single kid is staring at me, but plenty are. I do a bobblehead move to catch the sweat droplet that's trickling down the back of my neck, but it's no use. That one's just the trailblazer. I know another is right behind it, and another and another.

I could burst into tears and run. But nothing marks you for life like crying in school, unless it's about a crush, or a breakup, or a B-minus, all subjects that have suddenly become cool to cry about this year. The only way out of this seems to be to sing and get it over with. But I promise myself, if I do this, if I get through this moment, then I'll never sing in front of anyone ever again. Because there are things that are Shira and things that are not Shira, and this is not a Shira thing.

My mouth has gone dry. I'm not sure if I'm breathing.

There's sweat behind my knees. I didn't even know knees could sweat.

It seems like Mr. Hoover has been holding that note forever. It hangs there, waiting for me. Mr. Hoover gives me a nod and plays it again. And finally, I start.

"Oh beautiful, for spacious skies, for amber waves of grain." I hear my voice, and it surprises me. Even though I'm shaking all over, it's not a disaster—yet. *"For purple mountain majesties . . ."* I make sure to say "mountain" and not "mountains," because Mr. Hoover always makes a huge deal that that's the right way. *". . . above the fruited plain."*

Something about the singing itself, the physical feeling of it, calms me down. It feels like taking a long stroke in a pool, feeling yourself propelled forward, in a smooth space where nobody can bother you. I sing, *"America, America,"* a little louder, because it feels good, the line of it, letting my voice free to go up there, and then come down softer on *"God shed his grace on thee."* One more line, one more line and I'll be done. *"And crown thy good with brotherhood, from sea to shining sea."*

I look at Mr. Hoover, and for a second I'm afraid he's going to want me to go on, to sing the second verse, which would be a disaster because I don't know all the words, just something about "pilgrim feet," which always makes me think of barefoot Puritans with big black hats and goofy cartoon toes.

But instead, he just drops his hands from the piano keys into his lap and smiles wide. "Thank you, Shira," he says. The room is quiet, and everyone is staring at me. I want to just run out of here, down the street, back home, up the stairs to my room, and never come out. I feel like I've just read the most embarrassing diary page ever written out loud to everybody. A diary I didn't even remember writing.

I run toward the door. I get as far as the second row, where my foot gets caught in a backpack strap. I manage to pull, drag, hop my way free and out to the hall, with the door crashing closed behind me. Then I drop down onto the floor, my back to the metal of somebody's locker, which I swear is rattling along to the pounding of my heart.

Inside, I can hear Mr. Hoover start up "The Star-Spangled Banner." And I listen as Dylan Scheiner butchers it, in at least three different keys.

Chapter 2

A Hat and a Mustache

On Friday morning, I dawdle my way toward the music room, stalling as long as I can. I tie my shoe. I check for texts. I free my hair from its scrunchie, then wrestle it back into something close to a ponytail.

I can always hope that when I get there, I'll find a sign reading:

PLAY CANCELED.

NO ONE HAS TO GET UP THERE ON STAGE AFTER ALL.

But no such luck. I can tell from the cluster of kids outside Mr. Hoover's room that the cast list is posted. Everybody's crowded around two little white sheets of paper tacked up on the bulletin board. Some kids are on tiptoes, others push forward, all trying to get a look. A kid named Sean lets out a whoop and squirts out of the crowd like a watermelon seed. He runs into the music room and comes out with two books that say "The Music Man" on them in purple letters. Then he races down the hall to spread the news. A lanky girl named Delilah shouts, "Mrs. Shinn!" and raises her arms in triumph.

I consider ducking into the girls' room to buy a little more time, but I put that idea away when I see Monica Manley and Melinda Croce prance in there shoulder to shoulder, whispering and giggling. I choose to avoid being in enclosed spaces with eighth graders in general, and Monica and Melinda in particular. And there's no use waiting. If there's a mirror involved, it won't be a short visit for Monica.

"Shira!" I turn and see Cassie running toward me. Her backpack is bouncing like a rodeo rider hanging on for dear life. "Come on! What are you waiting for?"

I wish I knew. I'm not even sure what I'm hoping for. But whatever it is, I need another minute before I'm ready to see it dashed to pieces.

Cassie shakes her head and runs toward the crowd. She plunges in, but I stay back, thinking. I survived the singing tryout. Somehow, I managed to stumble through the reading audition, but only because one of the monologue choices was Sally Brown's speech from "It's the Great Pumpkin, Charlie Brown!" which I watched about a hundred times when I was five.

All I have to do now is go up and look at the cast list.

I take a deep breath, count to ten, and creep up to the

back of the crowd. Then I let the new arrivals jostle me forward and carry me in gradually, like a rock washing up on
shore.

Someone has crossed out the "BROOK" in Hedgebrook and written in "HOG." No surprise. Then, listed
first, are the leads:

HOG!
HEDGE~~BROOK~~ MIDDLE SCHOOL FALL MUSICAL

Meredith Willson's *THE MUSIC MAN*

Professor Harold Hill   Paul Garcia

Marian Paroo   Monica Manley

So that explains Monica's whispers and giggles. It makes
sense. She's the obvious choice for the lead, an eighth grader
who takes voice and dance lessons. I've even heard some of
the girls say in awed tones that she auditions for commercials in "The City." That's New York City. And anything that
happens in "The City" has to be way better than whatever we
do here in Hedgebrook.

I muster my courage and scan the first page, looking
for my name. I see the mayor's wife—that's Mrs. Shinn—and
someone or something called Amaryllis. I see Cassie's name
on the second page. She's a townsperson. There are River

City Ladies and band members and someone named Ethel Toffelmeyer. But my name isn't next to any of those roles. It's not anywhere.

I should feel relieved. I promised myself I'd never sing in front of anyone ever again, and now I won't have to.

But Cassie has been telling me all week how Mr. Hoover's face lit up when I sang, how I sounded really good, and how I could surprise everyone and get a big role. And when someone keeps saying something, even if it's crazy, a little part of you starts to half believe it. Or maybe hope it. Or maybe be terrified of it. Or maybe all three.

I look at the second page one last time, and then, far down, at the very end, I see it:

The Barbershop Quartet

Mr. Ewart Dunlop   Vijay Mehta

Mr. Olin Britt   Jason Chen

Mr. Oliver Hix   Felix Owen

Mr. Jacey Squires   Shira Gordon

"Hey, Shira," says a boy I recognize from math class. "You're a guy."

I pretend not to hear, because there's no point denying it. It's right there in black and white.

"My mom made me watch the movie," this kid goes on. "There are these four dudes with matching hats and mustaches who sing all the time. '*La-la-la*,'" he demonstrates, just in case I don't know what singing is. "You're totally playing a guy."

I stare at my name and try to come up with some other explanation: Maybe it's Ms. Jacey Squires. Maybe I'm somewhere else on the list, and this is just a mistake. I look again, but there's only: "Mr. Jacey Squires . . . Shira Gordon."

I tell myself it's not so bad. It could be a lot worse. I could be playing the rear end of a mule, or an old hag with missing teeth, or the town drunk. I could be asked to die a horrible death or dance in a tutu. It's not that unusual for a girl to play a boy's part. And it's not like I'm some super girlie type who only talks about nail polish and shoes. When I was little, my dolls sat on the shelf while I played with my toy dinosaurs, and I loved my Captain America Halloween costume in third grade. Still. It's not third grade anymore. It isn't even sixth. This is seventh grade, when people notice you. For all the wrong things.

Cassie was right. I did want to be in the show. In the back row, maybe. A villager among villagers. Wearing a pretty costume. But there won't be any fluffy skirt for me. No ruffles. No frou-frous. Not a single, solitary frou.

There's a sign in big letters telling us to pick up our scripts and scores in the music room, but I don't. My ears are starting to burn, and I know soon I'll be in full Shira blush mode. I turn away from the list and look for Cassie.

"Good luck with that," chuckles the "la-la" kid as he runs down the hall—probably on his way to spread the word to the whole seventh grade that Shira Gordon is playing a guy.

DID YOU LIKE THIS BOOK? CHECK OUT THESE OTHER GREAT READS.

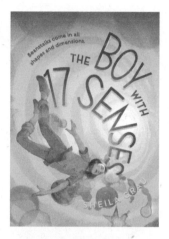